It rang four times. Six. Eight.

"C'mon, Grace," she muttered, her breath billowing from between chattering teeth, "pick up the damned phone."

A dozen times. Fourteen.

Jenny's throat felt tight when she hung up and tried again. Still no answer.

What could be wrong? she wondered, glancing toward her house. It was so dark, though, there seemed to be no house there at all.

"Oh, Lord," she said aloud, depositing the quarter again. "Oh, Lord…"

…inside the truck stop, Bill and Byron approached Adelle, Doug and the girls in the travel store and Bill explained what Byron had done.

Doug took Bill's arm and led him away to a rack of black Harley-Davidson teddies. Byron followed.

"Listen," Doug whispered firmly, "I'm not sure exactly what's going on here, but if this is some kind of prank, a hoax to get your wife back, or something, I'll throw you into court so fast you'll wish it had never crossed your mind."

Bill started to speak, but Byron beat him to it: "Hey, friend, if this is a hoax, it's got Allen Funt beat all to hell. Besides, I would've kicked the shit outta this guy by now, he was trying to pull something over. But it's no hoax and we ain't got no time to deal with you right now."

"It's okay, Byron," Bill said calmly. "Look, Doug, all I want to do is save my son, okay?" In a whisper, he added, "If that's still possible. Afterwards, you'll never see me again. I swear."

Doug softened then, averting his eyes a moment. "It's just… the whole thing is so—"

"—yeah, crazy, I know," Bill interrupted. "But we've gotta live with it." He slapped Doug on the shoulder and turned to Byron, nodding toward the restaurant as he said, "Let's go…"

LOT LIZARDS

BY RAY GARTON

DEDICATION

L ot Lizards was written mostly at the coffee counter in the late-night/early-morning hours in the 76 Truck Stop in Redding, California, where I first heard the term "lot lizard." As soon as I learned what it meant, I opened my notebook and started writing this book. It was at that truck stop that I met Dawn, my wife. No, of course she wasn't a lot lizard, she was working the graveyard shift in the gift shop. That was in 1987, and by the next year we were living together, and in two years we were married in a double ceremony with Dawn's widowed father. We've been together ever since. This novel is dedicated to her with love … and a little nibble.

PROLOGUE

When Bill Ketter walked out of the restaurant at the Petromo Truck Stop in Springfield, Missouri, after a meal of chicken fried steak, mashed potatoes and gravy, corn on the cob and a slice of lemon meringue, he was just tired enough for his limp to show as he crossed the back lot to his truck. His left leg was an eighth of an inch shorter than his right; he was usually able to hide it with a swagger, but when he got tired, the limp was noticeable. He hitched himself up into the cab of his eighteen wheeler and pulled the door shut behind him, ready to settle down for a few hours of much needed sleep when he heard the knock. Actually, he'd been hoping for it.

It had been a long trip from California to Illinois, and now he was on his way back with a load of furniture. But other than to make his delivery, Bill could think of no good reason to return. His wife, A.J., had left him six months earlier, taking their two children with her. He'd spent a few months waiting for her to come back like she always had before; she'd left him three times in the past, always for the same reason: she could no longer live with a man who made his living spending nearly all of his time on the road delivering everything from produce to kitchen appliances, and almost none of his time with his wife and children. But she'd always come back in two or three weeks—maybe a couple months.

She hadn't come back this time. It had taken Bill a while to realize that she wasn't coming back this time. He was feeling depressed, lonely and rejected—Admit it, he thought, you're feeling horny!—and that knock was like a sound heard by a man who thought he'd lost his hearing forever.

Earlier that evening, when he'd pulled into the truck stop,

that knock—or one like it—had been on his mind. He'd decided he needed something to take his mind off of A.J., and a lot lizard—one of the young women who roamed the back lots of truck stops, making a few bucks by going from truck to truck and knocking on the doors until they found a driver who was feeling lonely—would be just the ticket. He felt a sharp pang of guilt for considering it because it felt like adultery, infidelity... cheating. But it was pretty obvious that A.J. wasn't coming back this time and Bill felt like a walking sore, an open wound; he needed a salve.

"Yeah?" he called, kneeling on the sleeper bed, untucked shirt half unbuttoned.

"Uummm...you, um... you want some company?" A girl's voice, thin and tremulous.

"Just a minute," he said, crawling over the bed and between the seats, into the cab, checking his back pocket for his wallet. He opened the driver's side door, looked down at the girl bathed in the sickly yellow glow of the lot's mercury lamps and breathed, "Jeez, honey..."

The girl stared up at him with wide, dry looking eyes beneath which hung grey half moons of flesh. She was probably eighteen or nineteen, although she looked some years older at the moment. Her long dishwater blond hair fell in flat strings past her shoulders; her cheeks, the color of dirty teeth, appeared to be sucked in below razor-sharp cheekbones. She wore a filthy old olive drab jacket that looked three sizes too big for her frail, bony frame and a pair of jeans full of holes and she stood shivering in the warm spring night, hugging herself as if she were cold.

Bill knew instantly that sex was out of the question. Even if she were a lot lizard—although he suspected she was nothing more than a desperate drug addict—it was obvious that she did not possess the energy to rut around in his sleeper.

He threw the door all the way open and stepped down beside her, saying, "You okay, sweetheart?"

"Well, I was just wondering if, um... y'know, if you'd like some...y'know, some company."

"Yeah, but you look like you need the company of a doctor, honey. You okay?"

She lowered her head and laughed breathily at the pavement. "Well, I'm kinda...hungry." Looking at him again: "We, um... broke down. We were stranded for a long time and there was nothing to eat and..." She shrugged, still hugging herself tightly.

"You need something to eat?"

She nodded.

He'd lost interest in sex all of a sudden, thinking of his oldest daughter...and of A.J. No one but Bill called her A.J.; he'd always thought it was kind of sweet. He hoisted himself back up into the truck, offering his hand to the girl. "Then you come on in here, sweetie, 'cause I got a bunch of goodies you're more than welcome to, okay?"

She nodded, took his hand and allowed him to lift her into the cab. She weighed nothing.

"I don't have much," he said. "Some chips, some jerky and a few MoonPies, but it looks to me like you could use just about anything."

She nodded, never taking her eyes from his as she settled into the seat behind the wheel.

"So, where'd you break down?" he asked, fishing through the glove box for the jerky he kept stored there.

"'Bout sixty miles south of here."

"In a truck? A car?"

"I was in a truck."

"Uh." He handed her the jerky.

The girl held it in her hand, staring at it as if it were something odd that she didn't understand.

"The chips're up here," he said, jerking his head toward the sleeper. Bill moved between the seats and lifted himself up onto the sleeper's bed, groping for one of the bags of chips. He found it, pulled it noisily toward him and began to back out of the sleeper on his knees when he heard the familiar snickering sound of a cassette being pushed into his tape deck. The mournful harmony of the Judds filled the cab and Bill started to turn around when the girl came up into the sleeper with him, crawling over his legs on all fours.

"Uhh...you didn't like the jerky?" Bill asked.

"Maybe in a minute," she breathed, settling down on the

mattress. Her face was two inches from his and her eyes seemed three times bigger, or more, than they had a moment ago; they were like polished pennies with flecks of... what?... red?... silver? It was hard to tell... the flecks of color seemed to change, shift, disappear, then reappear. Her lips were dry and cracked and her skin, up close, appeared to be flaking. She'd probably been very pretty before she'd started taking whatever she was taking, hit the road and let herself go like this; she could probably be pretty again with a few good meals, a hot bath and some decent clothes.

"I thought you were hungry," Bill said, surprised by the softness of his voice.

"Well, really I'm kinda thirsty, y'know? My mouth is really dry."

"Oh, okay. Well. I got a jug of water in here, and some cranberry juice. And I think I got some Squirt left." He set aside the bag of chips and began searching around for the warm cans of soda when she touched his arm.

"It can wait," she whispered.

"Huh?" He turned to her again. "But I thought you were thir—"

She placed her hand on his cheek and leaned even closer to him and the colors in her eyes held his attention in an iron grip as she said, "I'm lonely, too."

Bill stared at her for a long time. When she pushed a fallen strand of her unwashed hair from in front of her eyes, he didn't notice; he'd forgotten about her hollow cheeks and unhealthy pallor. All he saw were her eyes. Such interesting, unusual eyes, and... in a strange sort of way... beautiful eyes. The flecks of color in them seemed to flare like dying embers coming to life beneath a gush of air.

"Know what I mean?" she asked, her voice a feather against velvet. "Lonely?"

Lost in those swirling flecks of red, copper and silver, Bill took a moment to grope for his voice, then: "Yuh...yeah, I...1-yuh...I thought—"

"Don't worry about it." She brushed her lips over his, soft as a butterfly's wings. "I'll eat." She buried her fingers in his hair and pulled his face closer as she ran the tip of her tongue along the curve of his jaw. "Eventually." Pulling away, she slipped her jacket off and began to unbutton the light blue shirt beneath it, smirking.

She looked different, somehow. Her eyes were brighter. There was something in her face, in the set of her jaw—a liveliness—that hadn't been there a moment ago.

Moving mechanically, Bill began to unbutton his own shirt the rest of the way, fighting back thoughts of A.J. and the kids, telling himself that he was lonely, he deserved—even needed— this, that surely A.J. wouldn't expect him to remain faithful to her after all these months of being alone, although he was quick to remind himself that, in spite of countless opportunities, he'd never been unfaithful to her throughout their marriage... and she still left! Despite his efforts, though, he could think of nothing but A.J. and his insides writhed suddenly with guilt until—

—the girl leaned forward, her shirt falling open to reveal small white breasts with chocolate-colored nipples standing erect, and slipped her hand under his shirt, stroked his chest and abdomen and began tugging at his belt, pushing him down on his back.

Money, he thought as she pulled his shirt off. She hasn't mentioned money...hasn't even told me her name...and...she looked so sick earlier...

But the touch of her hands pushed those thoughts from his mind and he trembled when, straddling him, she kissed his chest and sucked his nipples between her teeth, then stopped a moment to place her ear over his heart. Bill felt her fingernails dig into his sides, looked down to see her eyes close; the tip of her tongue glistened between tightly closed lips and she began to move on him, slowly at first, pressing her pelvis to his, then harder and more rhythmically, grinding against him as she sighed, "Aahhh-hahh...aahhh-hahh..." He became erect immediately and responded, pushing his erection up between her legs.

The girl moved down him, pulling his belt frantically, ripping his jeans open and jerking them down, pulling his boots off with them, then removing her own shoes and jeans, until she was naked. She crawled up his body like a stalking cat, her gaze fastened on the bulge in his briefs. She put her mouth over it, nibbled it through the material, making Bill squirm.

He was thinking of nothing now, not A.J. or the kids or his work or what he was going to do without his family... nothing. Just her mouth, hot and wet, on his cock...just her strangely cool, satiny skin against him...

Bill was startled when she made a sudden jerky movement and he looked down to see that she'd ripped his white cotton briefs off him in one quick movement; they dangled, tattered, from her clenched teeth until she tossed them aside and plunged her mouth over his erection, moving her head up and down rapidly, holding his testicles snugly in her hand, slipping a finger down to his rectum and pressing gently, teasing him.

He moaned and clawed at the blankets.

The Judds sang on, a different song now...a favorite of A.J.'s... but Bill didn't even hear it; he was swimming in the wonderful wet things the girl was doing to him with her mouth.

She finally mounted him, sitting upright as she moved on him at first, then leaning down to hold his face between her hands and kiss him...to clutch his shoulders as she bit his ear... then his cheek...then, quite suddenly—and, for just an instant, painfully—his neck...

Then something happened that made Bill lose control. The girl's vagina closed tightly around his cock, squeezed it like a fist, and she began to groan—no, no...it was almost a low growl—as she gnawed his flesh, sucking and sucking, her fingernails drawing thin trails down his shoulders and arms as she dragged her hands over him. The three sensations together—being inside her, the clawing of her nails, her teeth and tongue on his neck as she sucked voraciously—were almost unbearable and Bill began to gasp like a man suffocating, lifting his hands to push her away for a moment, to get her to slow down, go a little easier, but his hands only trembled uselessly and his arms flopped back onto the bed as he gulped, "My guh-gawd, muh-my gawd..."

His ecstasy crescendoed and his upward thrusts became

harder and more rapid and the girl made sounds just below his ear…thick, muffled sounds…sticky, wet sounds…and then—

—the truck began to move. Or so it seemed. It did not feel like it was moving backward or forward but… around. It seemed to turn slowly, like a carousel when the ride first begins. Bill gripped the mattress in his fists and tried to sit up, but his upper body would not respond. He made incoherent sounds in his throat as he tried to push the girl off, but she seemed not to notice. Her movements continued without pause and the sounds she was making grew louder, more intense, accompanied now by sloppy gulping and ecstatic humming: "Mmm-hmmm, mmm-hmmm, mm-hm, mm-hm…"

Bill opened his eyes to discover that the truck was not actually moving, but the sleeper seemed to be spinning, faster and faster, and the music on the tape deck grew faint, as if the volume were being turned down slowly; even the girl's sounds began to fade until all that was left was the feeling of sliding in and out of her cool wet flesh and, in Bill's ears, the ocean-like rush of his ragged breathing and the beat of his heart.

He began to flail his arms, tried to speak, tried to tell her to stop, to get off him because something was wrong, something was very wrong, but he could not utter a sound and his movements were weak.

The girl's movements, however, became more frantic and her hands clutched at him like steel claws.

At first, Bill thought he was having a heart attack. He began to feel cold, weak; what little he could see in the dark sleeper blurred and faded as did the sound of his heartbeat.

The girl either ignored or did not notice his distress.

His sight left him.

He stopped moving.

Bill Ketter slipped silently into oblivion…

Consciousness returned agonizingly slowly.

Bill rose from the utter blackness of a death-like sleep to the softer darkness of his sleeper, illuminated only slightly by the lights outside the truck. But that glow, however faint, had the effect of hot needles being plunged into his eyes as he opened them. He lifted a hand to his face protectively, uttering a throaty gurgling sound as he tried to sit up.

His whole body trembled as if from a tremendous hangover; a rank, viscous fluid coated the inside of his mouth and gummed up the corners of his aching eyes; gooseflesh crawled over his naked body like an army of ants and he hunched forward with a shudder, trying again to open his eyes, slowly this time.

He was alone in the sleeper, which was not unusual. But something about it was...wrong somehow. He looked around in the darkness, scrubbing his face with weak hands. The only time he wasn't alone in the truck was when A.J. came with him, but she hadn't come along on a run in... well, in years, so why did it seem odd that—

A. J.'s gone, a faint voice whispered in his head, which began to throb suddenly with the realization that his wife had left him. He massaged his temples, clenched his eyes and ground his teeth against the pain.

A.J. was gone, but someone else was gone, too, he was certain. Someone else had left him alone, but he couldn't remember—

The girl, he thought, opening his eyes. Squinting against the searing glow from outside, Bill looked down into the cab at the digital clock on the dash. It read four-forty a.m., nearly eight hours since he'd let her into the cab. Groping for his pants, his hand fell, instead, on his open wallet. He lifted it close to his face, fingers prying open the pockets.

His money was gone. So were his credit cards.

He dropped the wallet and grabbed his pants, making his way unsteadily out of the sleeper and into the cab where he put on his pants carefully, trying not to succumb to the dizziness that threatened to topple him. He started out of the truck, but froze when he noticed that his tape deck was gone. So was the small television he kept in the passenger seat.

"Son of a bitch," he slurred, clutching the seat to hold himself up. He threw open the door on the driver's side and started to step down cautiously, but the black pavement below flew up to meet him, striking him with the sound of thunder. The throbbing in his head worsened as he rose up on all fours, groaning. The sounds of the lot—once so familiar that he hardly noticed them—now drilled into his ears with barbed steel bits. Bare-chested, he hunkered on the pavement and looked around through bleary aching eyes.

Truck engines purred all around him like giant cats and the air was thick with diesel exhaust mixed with the smell of cow shit; the truck parked beside his held a trailer full of cattle. Headlights blinded him as they flashed by and he could feel the movement of the great rolling tires through the pavement beneath his bare hands.

He fell on his side and curled his knees up to his chest. Something was wrong, terribly wrong... he was sick, seriously ill...he needed help, he needed—

His stomach clenched and he began to retch. The meal he'd eaten in the restaurant earlier rolled up from his stomach in thick gobs and landed on the pavement, undigested and reeking.

When the tremors in his gut had stopped, Bill sat up and stared through watery eyes across the aisle between the rows of parked trucks to the next row facing him. One of the trucks was idling loudly. Its headlights were on and Bill squinted against the painful glare, but he did not close his eyes because... something was moving in the light...someone...

He sat up weakly, his chest heaving.

A slender figure stopped in front of one of the headlights, silhouetted against the glow. The figure hunched to light a cigarette; the head leaned back to exhale smoke and—

—a fist clenched in Bill's chest. His back straightened and his head craned forward as—

—the figure became more familiar, its identity given away by the curves outlined in the light, by the careless posture and the stringy hair that fell from the back of the head...

"C'mon!" a male voice called. "Whatta y'waitin' for, huh? Y'think I got all night?"

"I'm coming, okay?" the figure shouted back.

Bill scrambled to his feet, trying to ignore the dizziness that sent the lot spinning in all directions beneath him and stumbled toward the girl standing before the idling truck.

"Hey!" he called as he staggered toward the facing row of trucks, his voice thick. "Huh-hey, you! You!"

The figure stiffened, turned toward him, then hurried out of sight.

Bill fell to his knees on the pavement between the rows of dormant trucks, trying to follow the girl with his eyes, but a bright flash of white blinded him and the bellow of a truck's horn filled the night; Bill crawled frantically over the pavement, saw the enormous tires of a truck roll by just inches away from him and crawled desperately toward the lighted truck, his nails clawing the tarmac, until his head butted into a thick, stiff leg.

He looked up.

A man, fists on hips, grey-shirted belly hanging over his belt, looked down at Bill with frowning eyes. "The hell you doin'?"

"I was—I'm just—there's a—"

The man kicked his left leg out and growled, "Get the hell outta here, y'fuckin' drrrunk!"

The man's foot caught Bill's shoulder and sent him backward onto the pavement, but he sat up immediately, just in time to see the man's back as he walked the length of his truck and disappeared behind it.

Clutching the truck's bumper, Bill lifted himself to his feet and followed the man, leaning against the trailer all the way. As he neared the back of the truck, he heard the man's voice:

"...many times've I told you, goddammit, I ain't got all fuckin' night to wait for you! I don't care what you're—"

Bill rounded the corner and saw the man facing the trailer's open door, shouting into its yawning blackness. The man froze; his head jerked toward Bill and his lips curled into a snarl. He was grossly obese and his face was broad and lumpy; his dark hair was greasy and receding above his enormous ears and what teeth were left in his head were stained.

"The hell d'you want?" the man growled.

"The girl," Bill gasped, leaning against the corner of the trailer. "The girl who was...just standing...in front of the truck..."

"What girl?"

"The girl...the one you were—"

The man slammed the trailer door shut and jerked the latch,

turning fully to Bill. "I dunno what th'fuck yer talkin' about."

Overcome with dizziness again, Bill staggered, slid down the corner of the trailer and landed on one knee as he wheezed, "No-no-no...the girl...I saw her...sh-she stole muh-my—"

The man slapped a meaty hand onto Bill's shoulder and pulled him away from the trailer, grumbling, "Go sleep it off, buddy." He slammed Bill against the truck parked beside them and headed for his cab.

Scrambling to his feet, Bill followed him, panting, "Nuh-no, n-no! Wait! Please! You were juh-just t-talking to her, you were juh-just—"

The man turned and faced him and Bill froze. The man's lips curled up around his dirty teeth and his tongue moved restlessly behind the gaps between them; his eyes were small and dark, buried in flesh like a pig's. He lifted a hand to his round belly and scratched himself through the taut material of his dirty grey shirt. "Tell y'what," he said; his voice was the sound of a clogged toilet. "You get away from me an' I won't rip yer fuckin' head off."

Bill tried to back away but only fell to his knees again, weak and dizzy.

The man opened the door of his cab and climbed in. A moment later, the truck's engine shifted into gear and began to move slowly out of the parking slot.

The truck was black, jet black, a 1980 Peterbilt. Its 1693 Cat engine rumbled with the power of a volcano and the refrigeration unit on the white trailer, the side of which read in black letters, CARSEY BROS. TRUCKING, gave a steady, hollow hum.

Bill dragged himself up and stumbled forward as the black truck rumbled slowly out of the parking slot. He squinted at the license plates on the rear of the trailer as the truck rolled away, but his vision was blurred and his stomach was churning again and he leaned forward, clutching his abdomen and retching. He staggered half way to his truck, then fell, curling into a ball on the pavement, dry heaving.

"Hey-yum...you okay?"

Bill looked up through tears at a red-haired freckle-faced boy wearing a powder blue shirt and black pants, the uniform of the truck stop's shop workers.

"You-um...you don't look so well, man."

Bill was frightened; something was definitely wrong with him and he didn't know what it was, but something told him to keep it to himself...for now.

"Fuh-fine," he gasped, getting up. "I'm fine, ruh-really."

"You sure? You look...well, awful pale. I can call somebody if—"

"No-no-nuh-no...really. I'm fine. "He tried to smile as he stood, clutching his stomach. "Just...flu. Thassall. Got the flu, I think.

"Aw, shit, man, that sucks. Y'know, they got some stomach stuff in the travel store if you wanna...sweet Jesus! What the hay-ell hap'nuh y'neck?"

"My...my..." Bill looked down at himself. The hair on his chest was matted and slick with something that was dribbling down from his neck. He touched four fingertips to his jaw...a little lower...felt more blood coming from two small punctures. "What... what the... what'd she do to me?"

"What? Who?"

"That...girl." He pointed to his blue Kenworth. "She came to my..." He pointed to the empty space where the black Peterbilt had been minutes before, "...she was just standing right... she said she was..." He touched the wound again; it was sore and he winced, hissing, "She bit me."

"Well, uh, I-yuh..." The boy was looking at him very oddly now, shuffling his weight from one foot to the other. " I don't know about no girl, mister. 'Cause, y'know, we don't let none of them girls back here, know what I mean? None of them lot lizards." He began to back away, squinting at Bill's face. "Thass, um...thass why you gotta pay to come into the lot, so's we can keep 'em out, y'know? Um, if you want, I can call a cop. We got security guards here, y'know, I can tell one of 'em you're—"

"No," Bill said, still touching his bloody neck. "No, that's... that's okay." He shuffled back to his truck, and when he looked back, the boy was gone. It took an effort just to open the door of the cab and he stood there a moment, still, silent, fingering his wound and listening... to something...something...

It wasn't another truck...it wasn't an engine at all... in fact, it was very close, whatever it was...

He got into the cab, slammed the door and sat behind the wheel for a few minutes, taking deep, slow breaths. The storm in his gut calmed after a while, leaving behind it a strange emptiness. It wasn't exactly hunger, and it wasn't quite a thirst, and yet...

He found the jerky the girl had left behind and lifted it to his mouth but, an instant before he took a bite, he gagged and dropped his hand to his lap, suddenly taking rapid breaths to keep from retching again.

Water. That would help. He found the container of water and lifted it to his lips, sucked in a mouthful and—

—his throat closed, spraying the water over the windshield and dash. He coughed and gagged for what seemed a long time, then put the jug down.

And he heard it still... that sound that seemed so close...so unidentifiable...

He rolled down the window and inhaled deeply, hanging his head limply through the opening. The sound was louder.

He lifted his head... squinted...

It was a thick rushing sound... a throbbing...

Almost like a heartbeat.

He turned slowly to his left to the truck parked beside his... to the livestock trailer that reeked of cow shit. Even in the poor light, he could detect the movement of the cattle through the round ventilation holes that lined the trailer.

Much to his surprise, he could even hear their breathing.

And the throbbing sound continued...

Westbound Interstate 40, just west of Williams, Arizona...
Christmas had ended nearly five hours ago and the interstate was a corpse. The lights of a truck scale just off the freeway-glowed like a lonely ghost in the cold dark night. Inside the scale shack, Officer Larry Hauff of the Arizona Highway Patrol sat before a noisy portable heater with his feet propped up on a rickety table reading an article in the Weekly World News;

it seemed a mummified Egyptian pharaoh was still getting erections regularly in a museum in Cairo. He read, chuckled, sipped bitter coffee from a Thermos, then read some more.

It had been a slow night and a cold one. As cold as it was, Larry knew it would only get worse; Mother Nature was gearing up for one hell of a winter blitz, all the weather forecasters said so.

He heard an engine slow and turned to see a blue Kenworth pulling off the freeway; it was hauling nothing—no trailer, no truck—just the stubby, sawed-off-looking tractor. Larry stood, slid the door open and stepped out of the shack into the bone-chipping cold pulling his coat together in front as the tractor veered around the scales and slowed to a stop. The driver got out, leaving the engine idling, and headed toward him.

He was a lean man, medium height, and walked with a swagger. At first, Larry thought perhaps he'd been drinking, but realized, after a moment, that the man had a slight limp.

"Morning," Larry called, his breath blossoming into a small cloud of vapor before his face. "Can I help you?"

As he came closer, his face hidden by darkness, ice crunched beneath the man's boots where small puddles had frozen in the night. His hands were in his back pockets and his elbows jutted at his sides; he wore no coat. "I hope so," he said, stepping into the glow of the shack's light.

Larry flinched. The man's skin was the color of dry bone and his eyes were so deep in their sockets that they were hidden in circles of blackness.

"I lost my buddy a ways back and I was wondering if he'd been through here."

"Your buddy?" Larry suddenly felt even colder and folded his arms tightly across his broad chest. Something was wrong with this man. He was sick or...on drugs, maybe? "Well...what's he driving?" The steam that puffed from Larry's mouth as he spoke obscured the man for a moment, making him look even worse.

"A black Peterbilt? Extended hood? A white trailer that says Carsey Brothers Trucking on the side?"

The skin on the back of Larry's neck shriveled. Something

wasn't right here, something was… missing…

"Um… yeah. Yeah, as a matter of fact he did come through here. About an hour ago, hour and a half. It's been slow, so I remember him, yeah. Probably would've remembered him anyway. He was hauling—" Larry's throat was suddenly dry and scratchy and he stopped to swallow. "—caskets. Had a load of caskets. Uhh… hell of a thing to be hauling at Christmas time, huh?" he laughed nervously.

The man nodded slowly, thoughtfully. "Yeah…caskets… yeah, that's him."

Larry frowned. The man seemed to be thinking it over, digesting the information, as if it were news to him that the Peterbilt had been hauling caskets, as if it were important. And something else… something that made Larry's scrotum whither like a walnut…

When the man spoke, no vapor appeared in the cold air before his face.

"You must've lost him a while back if he's that far ahead of you," Larry said.

"Yeah, well…we got separated. How far to the next truck stop, do you know?"

Larry cocked his head, amazed: no steam, no airy white whisps from the man's mouth. "Truck stop? Uuhh…sixty miles. Seventy. Maybe more. Hey, um, aren't you cold, fella?"

He shrugged. "Had the heater blasting in the truck."

"Uh-huh. You know…you don't look well, if you don't mind my saying. I think it might be a good idea if you took a break, stayed off the road a while. I got some coffee here in the—"

"No. I've gotta go. But thanks." He started to turn.

"No, really. I'm serious." He tried to sound authoritative, but couldn't find any authority in himself at the moment. His stomach was fluttering nervously. "I don't think you should be driving."

The man faced Larry, took a step toward him…another step… still another, until the light peeled away the darkness hiding his eyes and Larry could see them. His own eyes widened, even watered a little as he stared into those…pits. When the man spoke, his voice was soft as melting snow:

"I'm fine, really."

The voice echoed in Larry's head as if in a yawning canyon: I'm fine, really, fine, really, fine, fine, really, really…

"You don't have to give me a second thought."

…ive me a second thought, give me a, you don't have to, a second thought, second thought really… "I'll be going now."

…going now' going, I'll be, now, going now, going…

"You go back to your paper."

…paper, go back to, you go back, paper, back to your paper…

The man stepped back. His eyes disappeared. He gave Larry a closed-mouth smile and nodded his head, saying, in a normal voice, "Well, I'd better head out if I'm gonna catch up with him. You stay warm."

Hands trembling, Larry nodded jerkily, smacking his dry, felty lips, trying to muster enough saliva to speak. Before he could, the man was climbing into his cab…revving the engine…driving away…

Thirty seconds later, Larry was seated in the shack again, sipping coffee as he read a story about extraterrestrials that abducted cheerleaders, chuckling and thinking about what a slow night it was…

CHAPTER 1

"Well, it's about time," Doug Purcell said as the traffic on northbound Interstate 5 began to move. There had still been some light in the steel grey sky when they'd come to a halt, but now Mount Shasta was blanketed by darkness. Engines fired up again and headlights flicked on, their glow reflected softly by the snow that lay all around. The windshield had fogged up for the third time and Doug swiped a hand towel back and forth to clear it before starting the car.

"I wonder what it was," Adelle said quietly. She sounded as if she were yawning, although she wasn't; it was sadness and fatigue that thickened her voice.

Jon leaned forward in the back seat and asked enthusiastically, "You think maybe it was a wreck?"

"Oh, Jon," Adelle hissed disgustedly, shifting in the seat as the car began to move slowly up the incline once again.

The boy leaned back with a sigh.

Ahead and to the right, Doug saw the blood red flicker of flares lined up on the freeway at an angle to guide traffic into the left lane. Fenced off from the traffic by the flares was a shapeless mangle of steel and shattered glass that had once been two cars. The red and blue lights of police cars throbbed and spun in front of and beyond the mess. It was the fourth they'd seen since they'd passed Redding. "Yep," he said, "it's a wreck."

Jon leaned forward again, barking, "Really?" and his little sister Cece uttered a small, breathy, "Oh…"

Adelle sat up and peered ahead. "Jon, stop it, okay? People could be hurt, here."

As they neared the wreck, Doug saw black splashes of blood

in the snow and a lone tattered boot standing upright on the freeway's shoulder.

"Oh, God," Adelle said. "Cece, don't look. Turn away."

The twelve-year-old groaned, "Oh, Muh-therrr."

Doug was slightly sickened by it all: the policemen walking about in their heavy coats and plastic covered caps with flashlight beams bobbing over the steaming blood in the snow and the monstrosity of twisted metal, the dome lights of their vehicles spilling the colors of tragedy over it all.

"Gaawwd," Jon breathed in awe. "I wonder if Dad ever sees anything like this when he's—"

"Jon, will you just shut up!"

Doug glanced back at Jon. "C'mon, son. Okay? For now? Your mom isn't feeling too—"

"Oh, please, Doug, please don't." She seemed to sink into the sheet, cupping a hand above her eyes as if to shield them from sunlight.

He looked over his shoulder at the boy again and shrugged.

Jon's arms were folded tightly and he looked out the window to his right as he mumbled, "Don't call me son."

A rustling sound came from the back of the station wagon. Doug looked in the rearview mirror and saw seventeen-year-old Dara, the oldest of Adelle's three children, sitting up, sleepy-eyed, among the luggage and blankets.

"What's goin' on?" she slurred.

Jon said, "S'just a wreck, dweeb, so go back to sl—"

"That's enough!" Adelle shouted, spinning around in her seat. "I don't want to hear another sound from any of you, do you understand?"

Silence.

Adelle settled back into her seat.

Doug looked at her again and his heart sank. He'd never seen Adelle like this and it hurt him, not because she'd been grumpy and snapping at everyone but because he knew that she was hurting. Maybe it wouldn't have been so bad if Jon hadn't mentioned his father...

"Next place we come to, I'm stopping," he said.

Adelle stiffened. "Why?"

"Well, for one thing, we could all use something to eat. And we need some chains if we're going to get there."

"We have chains."

"I said I'm sorry, sweetheart. I thought they'd fit your car but they don't and they're not doing any good. What do I know about chains? I'm a San Francisco boy. I've never driven in snow in my life."

"Well, I have. That's why I don't understand why you insisted on driving me to—"

"I didn't like the idea of you making the trip alone."

"I've made this trip a million times."

"Well, not since you've known me, and certainly not under these circumstances."

She scrubbed her face, making a sound halfway between a sigh and a groan. "They said she might not make it through the night. I wanted to…I just didn't…I don't want her to go before—"

"I know, honey." He reached over and squeezed her arm. "But we can only do the best we can. We can't control the weather or traffic."

As if on cue, it began to snow again.

They'd left Sacramento shortly before noon—less than two hours after Adelle had learned that her mother in Grants Pass, Oregon, had suffered a massive stroke—knowing the weather would be bad, but not suspecting that it would get so much worse.

Doug continued, trying to sound cheerful: "We'll stop, stretch our legs, have some dinner and find out where we can get some chains that'll fit. Okay?"

Adelle was rubbing her eyes with her knuckles; either she hadn't heard him or she was ignoring him.

He drove on, slowly and carefully, and after a while the traffic began to thin out. As they reached the mountain's summit, the freeway became less crowded and Doug was able to pick up speed a little—not much; he didn't want to push his luck—and the atmosphere in the car seemed to thin just a bit.

Below the mountains they'd just scaled, the small town of Yreka was nestled in a hilly valley and Doug felt much safer to be driving on flatter ground. A gentle glow—from the town,

Doug supposed—rose above the tall trees up ahead to the left and it was such a welcome sight, so pleasant to look at, that he almost missed the sign to the right of the freeway:

• • • RELIEF AHEAD • • •

SIERRA GOLD PAN
TRUCK STOP
FAMILY RESTAURANT - HOME COOKING
VIDEO ARCADE - TRAVEL STORE
GAS - DIESEL
FULL SERVICE - TRUCK & AUTO

• • • NEXT EXIT • • •

Doug relaxed a little; it was exactly what they needed. "Okay, that's where we're going," he said, nodding toward the sign.

Jon sat forward again: "Aw-right! I been there! Dad took me once when we—"

"Please, Jonathan," Adelle said, teeth clenched, "not in my ear."

Doug smiled, trying to loosen things up a bit. "Everybody just hang on a few more minutes. We'll all feel better after a... after—"

A tan Bronco roared past them on the left, its fat tires kicking up slush.

"Sonofabitch!" Doug growled. "Who the hell do they think they—just because they've got four-wheel drive, they think—I mean, there's still ice all over the damned ro—"

"Doug!" Adelle slapped her hand on his thigh and dug her fingernails in.

Jon made a pathetic, frightened sound in the back seat.

The Bronco swerved in front of them without warning.

Doug's entire body stiffened and he barely caught in time the urge to slam his foot onto the brake when he saw the Bronco's brake lights glare like angry eyes.

The Bronco began to fishtail as Doug feathered the brakes and—

—the small space between the station wagon and the Bronco was swallowed up in an instant and—

—Doug's foot pressed down hard and—

—the Bronco's brake lights winked off as the tan monster began to speed away ahead of them, but—

—it was too late.

The whole planet seemed to lurch as if torn from its orbit as the station wagon spun round over the freeway, a long clumsy top hissing over the snow and ice, zigzagging at first, the steering wheel taking on a life all its own, jerking from Doug's hands, which had grown slick with sweat, and—

—Adelle screamed, then Cece and Dara, and Doug cried out, too, like a child with a deep voice, as—

—the car tilted, ploughing through the snow to the right of the freeway as—

—an overnight bag was launched from the rear of the station wagon, clubbing Doug on the back of the head so hard that his vision vibrated blearily for a moment, until—

—the car struck something with a cry of torn metal and something under the hood began to hiss like a provoked snake and, for several minutes after the car had stopped moving, Adelle continued to scream and scream…

CHAPTER 2

The Sierra Gold Pan Truck Stop was usually a chaotic mess in the thick of winter, but on this night it was busier and more crowded than it had been since the infamously brutal winter of 1969 when the snowfall had been so severe that half of the roof on the Ten Pin Bowling Alley in Yreka, just eight miles north, had caved in and power had been down in the area for three days straight.

A line of trucks clogged the truckers' entrance and the auto parking lot was overfull with cars parked in NO PARKING areas, double parked, and still others illegally parked on the road in front.

The secured truck lot in back, which held two hundred trucks, had already taken in fifteen more than that and there were trucks parked haphazardly across the street and in turnouts along the road on the other side of the freeway, their lights glowing and engines idling as the drivers walked through the snow to the restaurant for coffee and some warmth.

A snow plow crept through the auto lot, zigzagging through the maze of cars as it scraped ice and snow from the pavement, its orange light spinning dizzily on top.

A lone trucker, shoulders hunched and stiff arms sweeping back and forth at his sides to fight the cold, opened one of the glass doors that led into the building's foyer and stepped into the crowd of people sitting around with arms folded and heads down, waiting for a seat in the restaurant or just…waiting… waiting for the roads into Oregon to open… waiting for a free payphone so they could make a call…

The building was shaped like a U. The foyer opened into the travel store, half of which was lined with shelves of gifts, souvenirs, T-shirts, sweatshirts, jewelry, jeans and boots, the other with automotive goods and electronics—citizen band radios, car stereos, portable televisions and handheld video games for bored travelers; in the back, a cooler held sodas, fruit juice and wrapped sandwiches and the register in front was surrounded by shelves of potato chips, candy and pastries.

To the left and around a corner was the restaurant, which had two coffee counters, one of which was in a section designated for professional drivers only. In the other direction and around another corner was the fuel desk, where truckers paid for their fuel and any parts and repairs. Beyond that was a laundry room and showers, free to truckers who purchased fuel and available to others for a deposit of five dollars. Also at that end of the building was the video arcade room, a bank of pay telephones and a lounge with a television for waiting truckers. At the end of the hall on the other side of a locked door, a staircase led to the management offices, all darkened and closed for the night.

On this night, the restaurant was so full that some of the people who just wanted coffee stood at the windows and stared out at the snowy parking lot as they sipped; others simply left their names with the hostess and wandered around the store or browsed through the magazines and paperbacks on racks in the adjoining corridor. The din of voices coming from the restaurant almost completely drowned out the twangy country music coming from the speakers mounted in the ceiling. But even the voices and the music were topped by the sudden sharp cry of a female voice and the thick, ceramic shatter of stoneware plates.

"Son of a bitch!" Jenny Lake hissed two seconds after her ass hit the wet floor. Her legs were spread before her, knees bent, as if her uniform—frilly white blouse, tight black miniskirt over black pettipantsand black stockings, which had earned the restaurant the nickname "Panty Palace" among the truckers—weren't humiliating enough. Bits of the three plates she'd been carrying surrounded her and the floor—as well as her shoes—were covered with spaghetti and meatballs, biscuits and gravy, and liver and onions. Her behind was planted in the middle of the puddle of water in which she'd slipped; it was cold through her nylons and she could feel her skirt becoming soggy and clingy. "Damn, damn, dammit!" she gurgled quietly through her teeth. This wasn't the night for it, it just wasn't the night.

Jenny's eyes rolled to her hand, which was spread flat on the tile floor, and saw beside it two feet in officious white sneakers. They were Dina's feet. Jenny looked up to see Dina standing with her hands on her thick hips, elbows jutting as she looked down with disapproval.

Dina Bonnick was the assistant manager in the restaurant. Dina Bonnick was widely despised. She was a petite woman in her fifties—somewhere in her fifties—with a tiny wasp-like waist and shapeless, rather lumpy, legs; she had a pale, withered face that was always too heavily made up and silverish hair that had been done in a strange outdated beehive sort of arrangement. She, of course, did not have to wear the uniform required of the waitresses and wore, instead, bright flower print dresses and beige stockings that were invariably wrinkled around her knees.

"Did you slip?" she asked in her quiet, pinched voice, after which her thin lips pressed together, emphasizing the wrinkles that branched out from them on the top, bottom and from the sides.

"Yes," Jenny said, getting up, "I slipped. I thought we were supposed to warn each other when there was water on the floor." She began to pick up the jagged chunks of broken plates and toss them into the trash.

"Those were orders, I take it?"

"Yes, they were orders."

Dina nodded. "They'll have to be deducted from your paycheck, you know." She cocked a penciled brow and leaned her head back just a bit in that way she had, almost as if she were daring Jenny to disagree.

"Yes," Jenny said, eyes closed. "I know."

Dina left and went back to one of the coffee counters where she'd been sitting, where she always sat; she never actually did anything, she just sat at the coffee counter sipping coffee… watching.

Jenny turned to go back to the kitchen window and give the

cook the orders again when she nearly ran into Kevin, one of the busboys.

"Sorry, Jenny," he blurted, stepping back, his fingers twitching nervously at his sides.

"For what?" she snapped, sounding harsher than she'd intended.

"The water. I spilled it. I'm sorry. Really. I was gonna clean it up right away, but…well, I…I'm sorry."

She shrugged, feeling a little sorry for the boy. He was taller than Jenny but seemed, somehow, shorter now. His boney frame seemed to have shrunk. His forehead was wrinkled beneath his head of wiry brown hair and his lower lip was tucked between his teeth. "That's okay, Kevin."

He smiled nervously.

"You might want to get a janitor to clean up this mess," she said, gesturing to the floor.

"Yeah, yeah, sure." His head bobbed frantically. "Yeah, I'll do that."

He turned and ambled away clumsily and Jenny went to the window and, once again, turned in the orders to one of the cooks, a stringy haired guy in his early twenties named Arnie Hamilton, who still had an acne problem and who made her very uncomfortable because he always stared at her breasts as he spoke to her.

Her bones ached, her head felt as if it had been clubbed and her feet hurt from the walk to work through the snow in the heavy awkward boots Grace Tipton, her landlady, had given her for Christmas. She was sick to death of taking orders, of putting up with the travelers' impatient remarks and put downs and the truckers' leering come-ons. She longed to go home to her little girl, to her bed and her electric blanket. But she'd just started her shift and it would be hours before she could do that. Shawna, her daughter, was home with Grace, who was probably settling down on the sofa now with a cup of tea to watch a movie or one of those damned tabloid news shows she loved so much.

Outside the foggy windows, it was still snowing hard: big fat flakes cut through by the headlights of still more cars making their way into the dirty slushy parking lot. The falling snow was rather hypnotic as it danced and whirled in the icy wind that, in the warmth of the restaurant, Jenny could watch without having to feel; in fact, for a moment as she stood there, she forgot that her feet, her head—her whole body—ached, and just watched the flakes, aware of nothing but her weariness... her miserable, leaden weariness.

Shawna loved the snow. She was probably staring out the window at the snow, too, about then, her splotchy grey face close to the pane, arms wrapped around Wendy, her doll, which was missing almost as much hair as Shawna...

'Table twelve," the hostess said breathlessly as she whisked by Jenny from behind, and suddenly the snow lost its soothing spell and the clatter and din of the restaurant returned as if someone had turned on a radio at full volume.

Table twelve was newly occupied by two large middle-aged men with snow clinging to their dirty hair and boots. Both were truckers; each had a log book on the table before him. She got two menus and went to the table.

"Coffee tonight?" she asked.

"One coffee, one hot chocolate with lotsa whipped cream," one said flatly, opening his menu.

The other looked up at her and smiled beneath an impossibly bushy mustache the color of nicotine stains and said in a gravelly voice, "Aw, c'mon, honey, smile. It can't be that bad."

She stared at him for a moment, stared razors into his eyes just long enough for his smile to shrivel, wanting to grab his plaid flannel shirt and shake him as she screamed, You wanna bet, Mister, you just wanna fuckin' bet it can't be that bad, you filthy, cocky, ignorant asshole? But, of course, she didn't. Dina was seated at the counter just a few feet away, watching Jenny carefully as she sipped her coffee, shifting her flat ass on the chair's cheap upholstery.

"A coffee and a cocoa," Jenny said, jotting the drinks down on her pad. "I'll be back to take your order in a minute—" Then, just under her breath as she turned: "—you miserable, cocky sons of bitches, you stinking unbathed road rats..." Feeling a little better after the silent tirade, Jenny sighed wearily as she brushed past Kevin...

…who breathed deeply to catch Jenny's perfume and slowed his pace a moment, closing his eyes to shut out everything else as he let her sweet smell embrace him. An instant later, his eyes snapped open and, cheeks hot with embarrassment, he glanced around quickly to make sure no one had seen him.

Kevin Bissette probably enjoyed going to work more than anyone else he knew, even looked forward to it on his days off, all because of Jenny. She spoke to him very little, and was sometimes even unfriendly, but there was something about her, something besides her looks and figure—her honey-blond hair and deep blue eyes, high cheekbones and slightly crooked mouth, and her legs…in those black stockings…hips hugged by those pettipants and that brief skirt—there was a sadness about her, a tragic sort of look in her eyes and in the way she moved sometimes that made her look so fragile, so vulnerable and in need of protection.

The thoughts he had about Jenny Lake were different than those he had about most other women. The things he found himself wanting to do with her were similar to the things he wanted to do to other women, but with Jenny, he thought it would be…nice. It would be slow and quiet and nice. No one would get hurt. Not like the things he'd wanted to do to that girl in lit class during his senior year—that Melanie Cormick, who had stared at him every day in class with that sneering little smirk on her lips and that narrow look in her eyes. He' d wanted to do to her the things her eyes had promised other guys on campus when she hadn't known Kevin was watching, but he'd wanted to do them hard so she wouldn't enjoy them; he'd wanted to humiliate her and wipe that look off her face. And his aunt Sylvia…her, too. But with her it would be different. She wouldn't be expecting it from him, of course, because he was her nephew. And with Aunt Sylvia it would be much worse, because that was what she deserved, and doing those things to her would probably hurt her the most. There had been others, but Aunt Sylvia topped the list.

He'd never done those things, of course, and probably never would. But he ran them through his head sometimes, saw them happening, heard the screams. That was enough. Kevin's imagination was always enough for him. He stayed away from girls, but he was good, close friends with his imagination, which was much easier and a lot less expensive.

Of course, Jenny was way out of Kevin's league, not to mention his age group. Kevin was eighteen and just out of high school, trying to decide whether or not to go on to college, while Jenny was probably pushing thirty and had a little girl—a very sick little girl, Kevin had heard—and even if they were closer in age, she probably already had more men after her than she knew what to do with, so what would she want with him? But at least she didn't treat him like Aunt Sylvia or Melanie Cormick; she treated him the same way she treated everyone else and he liked that. Someday, when he had a good job and enough money and was out of Yreka, maybe he'd be able to find someone like Jenny, someone with whom it would be nice.

He cleared a table in the corner, glancing over his shoulder now and then at Jenny as she filled a cup with coffee. What was it about her? What made her look so...forlorn? So lost? Like a little girl who'd been separated from her mother in a shopping mall, almost. He nearly dropped a plate as he looked over his shoulder one more time and earned a sharp glare from Dina Bonnick, which was enough to make him decide to ignore Jenny for a while...but not enough to make him stop thinking about her.

With his tray filled with dirty dishes and utensils, Kevin spun around and almost ran into Byron Quimby, the janitor...

...who stepped back quickly, light on his feet in spite of his size.

"'Scuse me, Kevin," Byron said with a nod.

Kevin smiled. "My fault."

"So, where's the mess?"

"Just on the other side of the counter, there by the coffee machine."

Byron nodded again, wheeled his bucket, mop and broom to the food scattered on the floor and began to mop up, all the while secretly enjoying the usual looks he got from the patrons, laughing inside at the sidelong glances, the whispering stares and the shameless wide-eyed gapes he got from some of the children.

There weren't very many black people in Yreka. Byron knew only three others. Byron was black. And he was big. Very, very big. The patrons, almost exclusively white, were usually somewhat startled when he walked into the restaurant and it took them a few minutes to adjust. This was due not only to his color but his size; his body was broad and solid, he stood head and shoulders above everyone else and was impossible to miss in a crowd.

Originally from San Jose, Byron used to be a trucker but grew tired of the road, decided he was getting too old to be living behind a wheel and eating bad food. He'd passed through Yreka several times and liked the area, found it quiet and relaxing, and decided it was the place for him. He had several acquaintances but no real friends, which was exactly how Byron liked it. He lived alone, which he enjoyed, preferring the company of books and music—mostly classical, which, for reasons he did not quite understand, shocked the hell out of nearly everyone he knew—and he spent much of his time making wood carvings of animals which he gathered up and sold each spring at the annual craft fair. And, of course, for entertainment, there were always the stares he got in the restaurant. They tickled him.

A short-bearded trucker writing in his log book at the coffee counter stopped and lifted his head slowly, frowning at Byron as if the janitor had just cut a raucous fart.

Byron stopped mopping for just a moment, cocked a brow at the man, then smiled and, ever so quietly, almost under his breath, just loud enough for the trucker to hear, Byron began to sing as he mopped: "Swing looowww, sweet chaaari-ah-hot, comin' for t'carry me hooome..."

The trucker belched and went back to his log book.

The country music playing over the PA system clicked off for a moment and a female voice called, "Janitor to the travel store, please? Janitor to the travel store?"

The trucker looked up at Byron again, less conspicuously this time, but Byron saw him and, as he finished cleaning up the mess, shook his head, smacked his lips and muttered, "Dey jes' ain't 'nuff hours innuh day," then wheeled his bucket, mop and broom away, still humming the song. He ambled down the corridor toward the store as the foyer door was pushed open to let in a man, woman, two teenagers—a girl and boy—and a little girl, all soaked through, covered with snow, shivering with cold and looking exhausted; the man had a large bleeding lump on his forehead and blood was trickling from the woman's lower lip. Byron stepped around them as they came in, nodded hello and was about to ask what was wrong and if they needed help, but stopped just short of stepping into the puddle of blood on the tile floor...

CHAPTER 3

When Doug opened the door and entered the travel store with Adelle and the kids, they were met with a bustle of activity which, at first, he thought had something to do with them. He knew better as soon as he saw the blood on the floor and the man with a jagged hole in the left side of his nose.

The station wagon was useless—he'd hit a fence post and the car was going nowhere without the help of a tow truck—so they'd walked the rest of the way to the Sierra Gold Pan, making a feeble and unsuccessful attempt to hitch a ride; all they'd gotten was splattered with slush. Surprisingly enough, the kids hadn't complained once about the cold or the walk or even the wreck; even more surprising was the fact that neither had Adelle. Not that she didn't have any reason to complain because she did, and Doug had been kicking himself all the way from the car to the truck stop for insisting on driving her to her mother's. In the future, he would remember this trip, tell himself that Adelle was perfectly capable of taking care of herself and would never let it happen again. At least there would be a future; he was thankful that, other than a few bumps and scrapes and one hell of a scare, no one had been hurt.

Doug had never been so cold in his life as he'd been on that walk and felt he might never be warm again; for now, he would be happy just to regain the feeling in his hands, feet and face, but when they entered the building, his own discomfort was forgotten as Adelle leaned against him, clutching his wrist and whispered, "Oh, God, what now?"

Cece pressed her face into Adelle's coat and groaned, Dara turned away and muttered, "Oh, guuhhh-ross," and Jon whispered, "Gaawwd!"

Doug felt a little sick.

The man, pear-shaped and balding with greying brown hair, leaned heavily against a change machine, his white-knuckled hands clutching the machine's edges for support. Blood was smeared over his face, darkening his green down jacket and had splattered the floor. The man's jaw was slack, eyes heavy, face pale and, although several people stood around him looking on with shock and horror, no one seemed willing to get near him; the hole in his nose—it looked more like a rip, actually—opened and closed repeatedly as he breathed, spraying blood and making a wet rattling sound.

An enormous black man who, for a moment when they first walked in looked as if he were about to speak to them, abandoned his mop bucket and rushed to the bleeding man's side, shouting, "Call an ambulance!" in a voice that could be felt as well as heard. He was joined by a tall thin blond woman in a dark blue smock who darted from behind the travel store's register. Wincing, she looked at the man's nose and said, "I'll get some ice."

"What happened?" the black man asked.

The bleeder's head rolled slowly from left to right. "A... fight," he rasped. "Flashlight."

"Huh?"

"Some guy...in the parking lot...hit me in the face with a flashlight."

Over his shoulder, the janitor shouted again: "Call the police, too!"

"Callin' 'em now!" a woman shouted from the fuel desk around the corner.

The store was crowded, but no one was moving; they all stood in a sloppy circle, staring at the blood and the man who had shed it.

The door opened behind them and Doug smelled the newcomer before he heard him—it was the rank smell of a fat man who had not bathed in too long—and when he spoke, his voice sounded like gelatin being sucked up by a weak vacuum cleaner:

"—up here for a while, then we'll—the fuck's goin' on here? Ho-lee shee-yit!"

Doug looked over his shoulder casually and saw the man: very fat, not very tall, thin dark hair greased back above a face like a gravel pit with teeth of rotting bark. The man he was speaking to was slightly taller, not quite as fat, but with the same hair; his face seemed to be sprinkled with a rash that, in places, was the color of ripe cherries. They were both so repulsive, they could have been brothers or, at the very least, first cousins. Both men stared in awe at the blood on the floor and the shorter, fatter one leaned toward the taller and, still looking at the puddle, muttered, "Get out there and make Goddamned sure none of 'em come in here. This'll drive 'em outta their fuckin' minds."

The other man nodded slowly, moved backward a couple steps, then turned and hurried out the door.

"A phone," Adelle mumbled, looking as if she might be dizzy. "We should find a phone."

Doug put his arm around her and turned her toward the restaurant. "Yeah, but first let's get a table and some coffee, huh? C'mon, kids." They shouldered through the crowd in the corridor until they reached the register where a young woman stood behind the counter talking on the telephone. "How long is the wait for a table?" Doug asked.

Putting her hand over the mouthpiece, she said, "About forty—" She stopped, looked them over and frowned. "Oh, Lordy, you folks haven't had a good night, have you?"

Doug chuckled. "I'm afraid not."

Leaning toward them, she whispered conspiratorially, "Well...let me see what I can do, huh?"

"You stay here with the kids," Doug told Adelle. "I'm going to see what I can do about getting a tow truck. Wave me down if you've got a table when I come back."

He wound his way back to the travel store, where the janitor was mopping up the blood; the injured man was gone, but had left behind a trail of red splotches on the floor leading across the store to a door marked OFFICE. Doug asked the cashier where he could find a pay phone and she pointed him toward the fuel desk and beyond but, as he turned, stepping around the janitor, he was nearly knocked to the floor by the fat, smelly man who'd been standing behind him earlier.

"Goddammit," the man growled quietly, hurrying toward the door.

Doug watched him grab the arm of a thin, pale girl wearing a long heavy black coat, who stood at the door staring open-mouthed at the janitor's mop as it slid back and forth through the smeared blood on the floor.

"Didn't he tell you not to come in here?" the man snapped, jerking her around and pointing her toward the door. "Now get out there, dammitall."

As if in a daze, the girl pushed through the door and walked slowly outside.

Doug turned and headed for the telephones, shaking his head and wishing, once again, that he'd never come...

By the time they were seated in a corner booth by the window, pinpricks of sensation were returning to Jon's toes.

"I'm seating you out of turn," the hostess whispered, "'cause you folks look like you need it, 'kay? Just kinda keep quiet about it."

Jon took off his coat, scooted over to the window and peered through the partially open blinds, hooking a finger over one and pulling it down; he watched the trucks outside as Mom ordered coffee and hot chocolate for everyone. She dipped a napkin in her ice water and dabbed her cut lip, then asked, "Everybody sure you're okay? Nobody was hurt?"

Jon and the girls nodded wearily.

There was a telephone at each table with a plastic card attached that read COLLECT AND CREDIT CARD CALLS ONLY and Mom placed a collect call to Aunt Janice in Grants Pass.

The waitress brought their drinks and menus, but Jon didn't open his. He'd been hungry earlier but had no appetite now. Being at the Sierra Gold Pan again made him miss his dad.

They'd come to the truck stop together six years ago. Jon was nine then and out of school for the summer so his dad had taken him along to run a load of sheetrock into Tacoma, Washington. Jon had ridden in the truck before—a dark blue and silver Kenworth that looked, to a nine-year-old, much bigger than it actually was—but he'd never gone on a whole run with his dad and he remembered having more fun on that trip than in Disneyland the year before. Probably because it had just been the two of them together inside that monstrous machine that sounded as if it were eating the road as they went. They could tell dirty jokes without a scolding from Mom; Cece, who was two at the time, wasn't bawling and getting car sick and Dana wasn't there to complain about everything. Just Jon, his dad and the truck.

And the stops they made! They ate at a restaurant that was inside an old train and stopped in Mt. Shasta where hundreds of people were gathered for a ceremony to worship the little men they believed were living inside the mountain; they visited a little town that looked like the set of a Western movie and Jon got his first taste of beer; and best of all, they stayed a night at the Sierra Gold Pan Truck Stop on their way back.

It was probably the least interesting of their stops and it wasn't as big as some other truck stops they'd gone into, but something about it had captured Jon's imagination. It was full of people—even in the middle of the night!—and had an almost carnival atmosphere that Jon found exciting. The engines of trucks made the parking lot pavement vibrate and disembodied voices called out names and made announcements in the night; inside, music played and voices droned and cash registers chattered and, in the back, a room filled with video games and pinball machines rang and beeped and buzzed Jon's favorite sounds. Dad cashed a ten-dollar bill and gave him forty quarters—not counting the ones in his pocket—and turned Jon loose in the arcade room while he took a shower; a few truckers had gathered behind him as he played and cheered him on to win three free games.

Now it was different. Without his dad, the truck stop seemed like just another truck stop full of weary travelers and overworked waitresses and cashiers. Everything was different without his dad.

"I told you," Mom snapped into the phone, "we'll get there as soon as—oh, don't start with me, Janice. The only reason for that is you live there. I'm a few hundred miles away and we've—because I can't afford to fly, that's why!"

Jon looked down at his hot chocolate and clenched his teeth.

He hated his mother's voice when she was angry or defensive; it was bitter and sharp, seldom raised but always cutting. That voice, Jon was certain, was the reason his dad had simply disappeared a year ago...

He turned to the window again, pulling a blind down. The snow was still falling heavily, thrown to the ground diagonally by the harsh wind. The road in front stretched to the right away from the freeway, flanked by streetlamps that glowed in the night like small moons. Some distance away, the road curved around a patch of trees and disappeared. On the outside of the curve and off the road a bit stood a large two-story house. A bright light shone in front of the house and a soft glow came from three of the windows: two below and one on top. In the top window, a small figure stood silhouetted against the light. A few moments later, a taller figure came, put two arms on the shoulders of the smaller, then both moved out of sight.

"Well, do they think she's going to get through the night?" Mom asked, her voice softer now and a little trembly, lips pressed closer to the mouthpiece, until: "No, we're not sight seeing, Janice, we had a wreck. I don't know how much longer we'll—Cece," she interrupted herself, "quit playing with the salt—I don't know how much longer we'll be here. We need a tow, then we've gotta get the car fixed and—oh, oh, yeah, here we go again with your favorite little guilt trip."

Jon rolled his eyes. Things were more interesting outside.

At the front edge of the lot, near the street, someone stood below one of the mercury lamps facing the restaurant. A girl. At least, it looked like a girl. She wore a long dark coat and its hem snapped around her legs in the wind; a cap was pulled down over her head and long fair hair blew around her face and neck. In the glare of the lamp high above her, the girl's face looked gaunt and very pale, as if her skin were caked with flour. She didn't move, just stood stiffly in the flurry of snow, hands in her coat pockets, watching.

Jon squinted, pulled the blind down and cupped his hands to his eyes, pressing his nose to the cold glass.

The window...she was watching the window, his window!

Just standing there as if she were unaware of the snow or the ice-cold wind…staring. At him!

"But what did the doctor say about the blood clot?" Mom asked, drumming her fingers noisily on the tabletop. "Did he say it could—Jon," she interrupted herself again, "Jon-athon! Leave the blinds alone." Into the phone again: "Did he say it could be fixed?"

Jon ignored her.

The girl still had not moved.

A truck rolled slowly across the lot and in front of the girl and Jon waited several seconds for it to pass.

The girl was gone.

His back stiffened, eyes darting left to right, but he couldn't find her. Where could she have gone? Only seconds had passed, not enough time for her to completely disappear. Unless she'd hunkered down behind a car…

The blinds rattled as Jon pulled them down further and craned his head around to look in both directions along the front wall of the restaurant and Mom hissed," Will you stop it!"

He pulled away from the window as she returned the receiver to her ear. "Of course David's there already, Janice, he flew. It's a couple hours from L.A. by plane. He's a lawyer. When I'm a lawyer with my own TV commercials, I'll fly, too, okay? Look, just get off it. What about Dad? How's he doing?"

Jon watched her; when she was staring at her coffee and chewing on a thumbnail, he knew she was too distracted to notice, so he tugged the blind down again and—

—cried out, clamping a palm over his mouth. The blind slapped back into place.

A white narrow face against the window. Full lips curled into a closed-mouth smile. And eyes…wide, smiling eyes… warm eyes… sparkling…

With her hand covering the mouthpiece, lips pulled back over clenched teeth, Mom rasped, "What the hell is wrong with you? Huh? Your little sister is behaving better than you!"

"I-I'm, I-I wuh-was—"

"Well, stop it." Pulling her hand from the receiver: "Okay, sorry, Janice. Just the kids. Look, when you talk to Dad, would

you tell him we'll be there as soon as possible? And tell Mom…
tell her I love her. Okay?"

Jon's hands were trembling from the jolt. Sitting across from
him, Cece was busy tearing up her napkin; beside him, Dara
was engrossed in the menu. Neither of them had noticed. Mom
was still talking, very quietly now, so quietly that he couldn't
make out her words above the noise of the restaurant.

He lifted his hand slowly and his finger quivered as he
hooked it over the blind and very cautiously pulled it down.

The face was still there, but this time, it wasn't a surprise.

It was the girl he'd seen standing across the lot. She gave
him a sly, playful smile and tilted her head forward a bit so
that she was looking up at him through long eyelashes. Her
frail white hand rose slowly and doubled into a fist, then her
long, slender index finger extended and curled…extended and
curled…beckoning.

Jon dropped the blind again, but only for a moment. When
he peeked out, her arms were folded and her eyebrows were
raised high. She mouthed silently, I'm waiting…

He slapped Cece's thigh. "Move."

"What?"

"I wanna get out."

"H' come?"

"I just want to, that's all, c'mon."

"Where are you going, Jon?"

He turned to his mom, still on the phone, and said, "I just
don't want to sit anymore. I wanna walk around."

"What do you want to eat?"

"I'm not hungry."

"Well, you better eat now, because I don't know when—"

"A cheeseburger. Order a cheeseburger for me."

"Where are you going?"

"Urm, just to see what Doug's doing." When Cece moved,
he scooted out of the booth, crossed the restaurant and hurried
through the crowded corridor to the front entrance, then went
outside into the cold…

CHAPTER 4

The hunger had been growing since he'd started driving at dusk.

So had the weakness.

The hunger began in his throat; the very first hint that he would have to feed soon was a harsh dryness in the back of his throat. A bit later, his skin became sensitive and he began to tremble just a little. After a while, his eyes began to water and burn and he looked as if he'd been crying. Then the chill set in; his body always felt cold to the living, but if he went too long without feeding, he began to feel cold and was soon shivering. His lips swelled and cracked. His skin began to flake. He'd never gone beyond that, but he was sure that, if he did, he would lose consciousness and, eventually, die.

Again and forever.

The weakness had started about four months ago. Actually, when he thought about it, he realized it had probably started before that, but he'd only noticed it four months ago. At first, he'd thought perhaps he was not feeding enough, or maybe he was doing something else wrong; his understanding of his condition was still limited. But even when he doubled his portions, the weakness persisted: a gradually growing heaviness in his arms and legs and a decrease in what had, for a while, been an amazing boost in his physical strength. Later, it had begun to show in his face. Added to the unhealthy pallor were heavy pockets of flesh that sagged beneath his deep-set eyes; his cheeks sank in further and further beneath his cheekbones over time, as if his face were deflating. His hair began to fall out, just a little at first, then more and more as the months passed. A couple of his lower teeth slowly began to darken and even loosen in the gum.

He had what he needed for his hunger in the back, but he couldn't drive while he was feeding and he couldn't afford the time to stop; it would sate his hunger for a while, but whatever else was wrong with him would only continue to worsen, slowly, steadily...

His truck idled as he waited for those ahead to move into the parking lot of the Sierra Gold Pan. Once in the lot, he drove slowly up and down the aisles. Unlike the others around him, he was not looking for an empty slot; he knew he wouldn't find one. He was looking for something else.

A black Peterbilt.

He knew it had to be there somewhere; the pass into Oregon was closed and no one was going past Yreka for a while.

It had to be there. He'd been looking for too long, following it too far to hit another dead end now.

Up ahead and to the right, he spotted it and eased to a stop: CARSEY BROS. TRUCKING. And just beyond it, he saw what he had been afraid to hope for: another truck identical to the first.

He'd heard about the second black truck about a week ago. He'd been asking around about the Carsey Bros, at a truck stop near Bakersfield; a young man on the gas island told him that not one but two trucks fitting his description had been through a couple days before.

So, there were two. And he'd found them both.

They stood dormant in the lot, dark and silent.

He looked around and saw a few truckers wandering through the snow, all men and none of them familiar. No pretty young girls with big eyes and milk-white skin.

They were nearby, though. Somewhere. Either hunting or feeding.

But with two trucks, there would be twice as many. And he was all alone.

Bill Ketter drove his truck out of the lot to look for a place to park...

Outside, Jon scanned the parking lot for the girl, but she was nowhere in sight. He walked along the front of the restaurant, hurrying by the window where his mother and sisters were seated and went around the corner. All he found were several cars illegally parked in a fire lane.

Maybe she was looking in the window at someone else, he thought. But he knew that wasn't true; she'd looked directly at him, smiled at him, beckoned him outside.

She'd looked about his age, maybe a little unhealthy, but… there was something about her… something exciting… something in her eyes that made him forget about his dad… that made him want nothing more than to rush outside and meet her.

Now he felt like a dork.

Cold as he was, he didn't feel like going back in yet; it was nice being alone for a while. He walked to a row of shrubbery, now covered with sheets of snow, that separated the front parking lot from the truck lot's exit and stepped up on the concrete edge of the divider. In the distance, where the road curved away, the windows of the house still glowed like stationary fireflies, but the small figure that had stood in the upper story had not returned. Somehow, that made him feel even worse.

Jon fished in his pocket and found a few stray quarters. Maybe there was an unoccupied video game or pinball machine in the arcade room. He turned and started back toward the front entrance when he heard the growl of a truck's engine beyond the row of shrubs. He stopped and looked back as the truck eased by, stopping at the edge of the road for a moment.

Jon frowned.

It was a Kenworth. A blue Kenworth tractor with no trailer.

He went back to the divider, hopped up on the edge and pulled two of the shrubs apart for a better look, knocking clumps of snow to the ground.

As the tractor pulled onto the road, Jon glimpsed the broad silver stripe that ran along the side of the cab and his breath caught sharply in his throat.

He pushed through the shrubs and hurried toward the truck lot's exit as the Kenworth crossed the road and pulled into a vacant spot on the shoulder.

Jon stood across from the tractor and watched, jaw slack, as the lights went off and the engine stopped. There was movement in the cab. Soft light came suddenly from behind the seats: the sleeper.

Moving cautiously, Jon started across the road, eyes locked on the driver's window. He stood beside the truck and listened.

Faint sounds of movement, but nothing more.

Jon's insides seemed to tremble with anticipation. There was no doubt it was exactly like his dad's Kenworth. But was it his Kenworth? He could find out.

Grabbing the handle beside the door, Jon stepped up on the running board carefully, quietly, and peered in the window.

It was there: the green rubber Triceratops his dad had bought him on their trip. Jon had insisted Dad hang it from the truck's rearview mirror and it had been there ever since.

"Dad," Jon whispered through a smile, opening the door quickly and repeating it, louder: "Dad! Hey, Dad!"

There was a cough from the sleeper, a wet sputtering sound and a shuffle of sudden movement. "Who's—what the hell's—" Someone stumbled down between the seats and turned.

A man.

His hair was mussed and spiky. His long face was white. And a dark thick liquid was smeared around his mouth and dribbled from his chin.

This man could not be Jon's father. But he was.

Jon fell out of the cab, screaming...

CHAPTER 5

Shawna Lake could lie still no longer. She listened for Mrs. Tipton coming back upstairs with her hot cider and, when she heard nothing, swept her covers aside, got out of bed and went back to the window.

The night was coated with sparkling sugar; flakes of it danced in the wind. But Shawna's enchantment was not evident on her face. In the frosty windowpane, her reflection was superimposed on the night like the face of a ghost. Her skin was grey and splotchy as tarnished steel; once chubby cheeks now sank inward and blond hair that had fallen to the middle of her back was now an inch or so long with bare patches where the hair had not yet grown back from the effects of the chemotherapy. On top of all that, she wore an intense frown.

Something was terribly wrong but Shawna did not know what; that was the reason for her frown.

While she enjoyed watching the snow from her bedroom window, she did not watch it now. She looked, instead, at the truck stop in the distance where her mother was working at the moment. She imagined Mom in the restaurant rushing from table to table in the uniform that they both thought was so silly. It usually did not bother Shawna when Mom left for work at night because Shawna knew how badly they needed money. But tonight it did bother her. Because tonight, something was terribly wrong.

The road was flanked by parked trucks, some with lights shining, others dark, like giant metal beasts napping for a while. One of the darkened trucks—a short funny looking one with no trailer behind it—was parked beneath a street light and Shawna saw someone climb up on it, open the door and lean inside.

A moment later, the person on the side of the truck fell backward onto the road and began to crawl, face up, away from the truck.

Shawna gave a tiny gasp as she clutched the curtain, then a startled little squeak when Mrs. Tipton said, "Here's your cider, hon—oh, I'm sorry. I didn't mean to scare you. You okay?"

"There's something wrong."

"What?"

"Something's...just wrong."

Mrs. Tipton put the steaming mug on the nightstand and sat on the bed, motioning for Shawna to join her. "What's wrong, honey? Do you feel bad? Are you in pain?"

"No, not me. There's somebody down there." Shawna turned to the window again and pointed.

"Well, of course there is. There are lots of people down there." Mrs. Tipton walked over to Shawna's side and put an arm around her.

"No, look. Down there. See? Someone fell off of that truck." She watched as another figure stepped down from the truck and approached the one on the ground, which was still crawling backward frantically. "And now that one there is—"

"Oh, you just come away from there, sweetheart," Mrs. Tipton said, turning her from the window and leading her to bed. "You don't need to watch all the goings on down there. Those truckers, sometimes they just forget how to behave in public and they start picking on each other. It's nothing you need to see. Besides, that window's cold. You should snuggle into bed where it's warm." She went back to the window and pulled the shade down, then tucked Shawna into bed, pulling the covers up around her chin. "Would you like some music? I can turn the radio on."

"Okay," she said softly. But her eyes were still on the shaded window, her imagination still down on the road in front of the truck stop.

Mrs. Tipton turned the dial on the radio beside Shawna's bed until she found some gentle, soothing music, then leaned over Shawna and smiled. She was a round woman with hair the color of wood smoke, sparkling eyes surrounded by little crinkles and false teeth that shifted and clicked when she smiled.

"Now," Mrs. Tipton whispered, stroking Shawna's cheek, "you think some nice thoughts and you'll have some nice dreams."

Shawna tried to smile as she nodded and Mrs. Tipton kissed her on the forehead. She left the bedroom door half open and Shawna could hear the stairs creak as she went back down to watch television.

But Shawna could not think pleasant thoughts and she didn't expect to be asleep very soon. Because something was still terribly wrong...

"Jon!" Bill hissed as he watched his son fall out of the cab and scurry over the slushy pavement like a crab. His insides shriveled when he saw the look of undiluted horror on the boy's face and heard his scream dissolve into a frightened whimper.

His feeding had been interrupted and he was still trembling all over, but he jumped down and rushed to Jon's side. "Jon, it's okay, Jon, really, if s—"

"Nuh-no, no, s-stay away, you're, you're...just...stay away." Jon stopped crawling and lay on the road staring up with wide, terrified eyes. The terror drained from them slowly, just a bit at a time, as he stared at Bill, and he finally whispered, "Duh... Dad?"

"Yeah, Jon." Bill hunkered down beside him, suddenly overwhelmed with affection, with the feeling of loss that had gnawed at him for a year now like an impossibly unappeasable hunger...but this time the feeling was magnified tenfold. He clutched Jon's shoulders and lifted the boy into his arms, holding him close, squeezing him so tightly that Jon grunted as he returned his father's hug.

After a long moment, Bill pulled back and looked at his son, his handsome son who looked so much more mature, so much older than he had a year ago.

"Oh, God," Bill whispered. "God. Jon, you're... you look so good, boy. You look..."

Still visibly shaken, Jon touched his own lips, frowning, and asked, "What…what's the stuff on your mouth?"

"Oh, shit." Bill wiped his mouth quickly and stood. "Look, Jon, just wait here a second, okay? Just…don't go away." He went back into the cab and climbed into the sleeper. His icebox was open, filled with clear plastic bags that contained his sustenance. He'd stolen them last night from a closed and darkened blood bank in Redding before parking for the night at the 76 Truck Plaza. One of the bags was open and half empty. He stared at it a moment, then licked the hand he'd used to wipe his mouth, closing his eyes and exhaling tremulously. He glanced over his shoulder; the boy had not followed him into the cab.

A little more. Just a little more…

Kneeling on the bed, he took the open bag in a quavering hand and put his mouth over the opening, tilting it back.

After the second thick gulp, he fell sideways, leaning against the wall as he was overcome by the brief weakness that always accompanied a feeding. It was a weakness that came from the inside, the weakness of ecstasy, of orgasm. But it was not as strong this way…feeding from an ice-cold plastic bag… alone…

It was always much stronger—intoxicating, mind altering— when it was warm and fresh, drawn straight from a living, breathing, struggling body.

Bill had only fed that way once and had not been able to bring himself to do it again. Not yet.

Even so, as he swallowed the last of it, he became aware of his erection, of the not unpleasant throbbing in his head and the tingling sensation that ran over his body in a wave, as if he were being covered, naked, by a blanket of feathers.

He wadded the plastic bag in a weak fist as he waited, breathing deeply, for it all to pass.

Afterward, he regained his composure, wiped his mouth and went back out to see his son.

Jon was staring up at the open door, waiting. He spoke hesitantly: "You don't…um, you don't…look so good, Dad. Are you okay? Are you—" He swallowed, licked his lips. "—um, are you sick?"

Bill looked at him for a long time, wondering how this could happen, how the boy could be here on this night. Were A.J. and the girls here, too? They had to be; Jon certainly didn't drive himself. After a moment, all of that became less important...

Jon was still growing, but he would be tall and his shoulders would be broad when the growing was done. Bill saw himself in the boy. The girls had gotten their mother's red hair and fair skin, but Jon had inherited Bill's face and eyes, his thick brown hair and olive complexion.

Leaning out of the cab, Bill extended his hand and said, "Come on up, Jon. We've got a lot to talk about."

CHAPTER 6

They smelled. Both of them.

Jenny wrinkled her nose when they stepped in front of her, making her stumble to a halt.

"We'd like a table," the fattest one said.

"Well...you're supposed to be on the list, you know," she said. "There's a wait."

Jenny was relieved when Debbie, the hostess, stepped up and said, "Can I help you?"

"We'd like a table," the fat, smelly man repeated.

"Well, you'll have to wait. We're pretty full, in case you didn't notice."

"How long?" the man asked.

"Maybe an hour. Maybe more."

The man looked at his partner, not as fat but just as smelly, and both of them smirked as they turned and walked away.

Debbie looked at Jenny and said quietly, "Some day I'm gonna come in here with a gun."

Jenny nodded with a sympathetic smile, then hurried to her original destination: a newly occupied table. She took the order without really listening, writing it down automatically on her pad like a robot, then turning to take it to the cook. Someone touched her shoulder and she turned.

"You gotta phone call," Debbie said, hurrying back to the register.

Jenny turned in the order, then went to the front and picked up the receiver behind the register. "Hello?"

"Hi, Jen, it's me. Grace."

Jenny's stomach lurched. "Is something wrong?"

"No-no-no. It's just that Shawna's...well, you told me to call if anything was unusual and... well..."

She clutched the receiver with both hands. "What, Grace?"

"Shawna can't seem to go to sleep. She keeps saying... well, she keeps saying something's wrong."

"What?"

"She doesn't say. Well, she doesn't know, I guess. She just keeps saying that something's wrong. I just took a cup of cider up to her, but she's still...she's disturbed. I don't think she's going to go to sleep. I just thought I should call. You know. I thought I'd ask you what to do."

Jenny closed her eyes a moment to think. Shawna had had trouble sleeping in the past, but never for a reason, never because something was "wrong." When she opened her eyes again, she found herself staring over the counter at the fat smelly men who had demanded a table just a few minutes ago.

The first one smiled at her, his fat cracked lips framing darkened teeth that were clamped together on the end of a stubby cigar; the other chewed on a wooden match. Between them stood a petite girl, maybe in her teens, pretty but pale and very thin, with blond buzz-cut hair that showed off the three delicate silver earrings that dangled from each ear.

"Is she there, Grace?" Jenny asked, looking away from the customers.

"She's in her room, but she's not asleep yet. I just heard her roll up the shade on her window. She just won't stay away from that window. She saw a couple of truckers fighting down on the road earlier and I think that upset her."

"Well...go ahead and put her on, let me talk to her."

"Okay, hold on."

The line fell silent and Jenny looked at the young blond girl again. She was talking to Debbie, staring intensely into her eyes, leaning close as if what she had to say was a terrible secret.

Debbie stood with her head tilted forward, lips parted and jaw slack, back straight and stiff, which was odd for her because she was usually smiling and always relaxed, sometimes so relaxed she looked rather slumped.

When Jenny looked at the man with the match in his mouth, he winked at her and she turned away quickly, looking at

Debbie again, who nodded and said flatly, "Sure, right away."

Debbie turned, scanned the restaurant, then motioned for them to follow her as she headed for a table where a man, woman and little boy were just standing to leave. But the girl did not follow; she turned to the man with the cigar, who nodded at her, as if in thanks. Then he said, "Watch yerself out there," and shouldered by her. The girl left the restaurant while the two men followed Debbie to the cluttered table, which she began to clear off without waiting for the busboy.

Jenny frowned. The only time she'd ever seen Debbie seat anyone out of turn on such a busy night was a little while earlier when that family had walked in soaking wet and bleeding from cuts and scratches after walking up the freeway from their wrecked car; usually, she was very careful to uphold the restaurant's first come first serve policy so as not to upset those customers left waiting for a table. And Debbie never cleared off a table without snapping at the busboy for not getting to it first. But now she took away the dirty dishes, wiped the table with a rag and poured coffee for the men, gave them menus, then hurried past the register and ducked into the restroom.

"Hi, Mom," Shawna said.

"Hello, Pumpkin. How're you?"

"Fine."

"That's not what Mrs. Tipton says. She says something's bothering you."

"Well…"

"What is it, honey?"

"I don't…really know."

"You're not sick?"

"Uh-uh. I just…I don't know. Are…you okay, Mom?"

"Of course I am, honey. Why, did you think maybe I wasn't?"

"I just…wasn't sure. That's all. I'm fine, though."

"Well…okay. Look, if you can't sleep, tell Mrs. Tipton I said you could stay up and watch TV, okay? And I'll call and check on you during my break."

By the time Jenny got off the phone, Debbie had returned to the register.

"Hey," Jenny said quietly, "how come you seated those guys?"

"What guys?"

"Those guys." She pointed to their table and Debbie squinted as she peered across the restaurant.

"That family? They looked awful and I figured—"

"No, no, the table next to them."

"I didn't seat those guys."

"Yes you did. I just stood here and watched you. They came in with some girl, a teenager, and she said something to you and you seated them. And here we've got all these people waiting to—"

"What girl?" Debbie faced her and Jenny could see that she was genuinely puzzled, confused. "I didn't talk to no teenage girl."

Jenny opened her mouth to argue but thought better of it; it was the look on Debbie's face that stopped her, that pinched look she got when she didn't understand something or thought someone was pulling one over on her.

"What the hell're you talking about, Jen?"

"I, um…nothing. Nothing."

Troubled, Jenny left the register and went to take the men's order, not looking forward to getting close to them again…

It was cold in the cab, but his dad did not offer to turn on the heater. He'd turned out the light in the sleeper so they were left with only the glow of the streetlight outside and his dad's face was hooded in shadow as he sat behind the wheel.

"So your mom's inside, huh?" he asked, looking toward the restaurant.

"Yeah. They're having dinner."

"The girls, too?"

Jon nodded and started to add, And Doug, but stopped himself. Dad didn't know about Doug. At least, Jon didn't think he did. Before Mom had packed up and taken them to live with Grandma for a while, Doug had always visited while Dad was on the road. Jon had wanted to tell him about Doug, felt it was only right that he know because, as time passed, Doug's visits became longer and more frequent and he and Mom spent more and more time alone together. But Jon had said nothing, knowing how his mother would have reacted, how she would have shouted at him and probably grounded him until he was thirty. Then, when Dad just sort of disappeared, Jon had wished he'd told him, just come right out with it no matter what Mom would have done. Maybe then the past year would have been very different.

"Who else?" Dad asked.

Jon was startled. "What?"

"Who else is she with? You were about to say someone else. Who?"

"Oh. Um. Well..."

"It's all right. You can tell me."

"His name is Doug."

Dad repeated the name softly: "Doug. Hm. Doug." Then he nodded as he stared at the restaurant's bright windows. After a moment, he turned to Jon and asked, "Does he live with you?"

Jon bowed his head, feeling ashamed, as if he had betrayed his dad somehow, as if he had asked Doug to move in with them himself. "Yeah."

"It's okay, Jon. Don't feel bad about it. Is he a good man? Does he treat you well?"

Jon shrugged.

"Oh, c'mon. He's gotta have some good qualities."

Another shrug. "I don't know. Things just aren't...the same."

"Things don't ever stay the same, Jon."

Looking into his dad's black face, Jon asked, "Can I come live with you? I could go on the road with you. I've only got another year of school left, and I could take a correspondence course. We could—"

But he was already shaking his head. "No, Jon. You've got to stay with your mom. She's really going to be needing you after Grandma dies. And just in case this Doug isn't such a good guy after all, she needs someone around to keep an eye on her. And you need to finish school with your friends."

Jon clenched his teeth as a surge of anger welled up in his chest, anger at the unfairness of his life. He had no control over anything around him; he wasn't able to make any choices for himself, they were made for him by others, whether he liked the outcome or not. Suddenly he didn't want to be with his dad anymore, even though he'd wanted for the past year to see him so badly. He felt like throwing a tantrum, the kind only children threw when things didn't go their way. He felt like hitting something, like shouting, like—

"Why the hell did you have to just disappear like that?" Jon shouted. His voice was deafening in the cab and his dad started. "Did you think just because she wanted to leave you that I did, too? You couldn't write? You couldn't call once in a while? Just pick up a phone somewhere and call? Other people are divorced, some of my friends' parents are divorced, but they at least keep in touch with their kids, you know? They call, they visit. But you, you just…you just disappear, like a fucking criminal, like you're wanted by the police, or something! And you look so bad, so sick, like there's something wrong with you, but you won't tell me anything, like where you've been or where you're going or if I'm ever going to see you again, and…and I…" His next words stuck in his throat for a moment, clogging with the hot tears that were burning there and welling up in his eyes. Lowering his voice, but still speaking with trembling intensity, he added, "I hate you for that. I've thought about you so much this past year, thinking you'd come back or get in touch. But I had to meet you here by accident, and if I hadn't I'd probably never see you again. And I really don't care if I do." He fumbled with the door's handle to get out but it was locked and he groped around to unlock it, saying, "Because I hate you. For leaving me with her and just taking off, I hate you, I hate you for—"

His dad closed a hand gently around Jon's wrist and Jon gasped, shocked by the icy chill of his dad's skin. He froze, looked down at the hand on him, so white, veins so pronounced, fingers so boney…then he looked at his dad.

He'd leaned forward and his face was in the light. He looked different than before and worse than Jon had originally thought. His skin, impossibly drained of all color, seemed to be stretched taut over his skull, showing every bone in his face but his eyes were now bright above half moons of sagging flesh, wide, more alive than Jon had ever seen them, but sunken so deep into their sockets that they seemed about to completely disappear.

AIDS, Jon thought with horror, unable to speak the word, he's got AIDS. He's dying.

"Please don't hate me, Jonny," he said in a whisper. "I didn't want to disappear. I've thought of you every single day since the last time I saw you. But I...couldn't see you. I didn't want you to see me. Not like this."

"What's... wruh-wrong, Dad?"

"Something's happened to me. I'm...different now."

"Do you have—"

"No-no, I don't have anything. Not...really. I guess you could say I'm not well, but it's not a sickness. Not exactly." He looked down at his hand on Jon's wrist and frowned, thinking, struggling with something.

"What, Dad? Tell me what's wrong with you."

"I can't, Jon. I just can't explain it, it's too...you wouldn't understand it. You'd think I'm crazy."

"No I wouldn't!" Jon hissed.

He was silent for a long time, so long that Jon began to think he'd just...slipped away, or something. Then he nodded. Looked Jon in the eyes. And speaking slowly and monotonously, he began to tell Jon what had happened to him in the last year.

As he listened, Jon was filled slowly with a fear much colder than the snowy night outside...

CHAPTER 7

As Kevin passed the order counter carrying a tray of dirty utensils, the cook, Arnie Hamilton, leaned out and called, "Hey, Kevin, we're almost out of cheese. Go down and get some, huh?"

Kevin put the tray down on the dish cart with a tray of plates and called over his shoulder, "What kind?"

"Both."

"No problem." He smiled slightly as he wiped his hands. He liked to go down in the basement; he was the only one who ever went down in the basement on this shift and it gave him a chance to be alone and take a few tokes.

Passing through the kitchen, Kevin grabbed a ring of keys from a hook on the wall. At the end of a narrow corridor that went all the way to the back of the building, he unlocked a rickety door, reached in to flick on a light and went down the steep stairs to the basement.

The fluorescent tube lights made delicate tinkling sounds as they flickered on and bathed the stacks of boxes and crates and shelves of restaurant equipment in glaring white light. It was damp and smelled of cardboard and wet cement and it was almost as cold going down there as it would have been stepping outside.

Across the basement from the staircase was the freezer's broad steel door. Kevin thought it looked like the door to some awful prison cell, the kind of cell reserved for only the most heinous offenders; sometimes when he opened it up, he imagined finding not the restaurant's food but a dark and smelly room with mossy stone walls to which were chained the decayed rat-eaten remains of prisoners who had been locked up and forgotten. Of course, there was nothing beyond the big steel door but meats, cheeses, ice cream, frozen batters and God only knew what else, but giving his imagination an occasional walk in the park made Kevin's job a little more enjoyable.

His feet crunched over the damp concrete floor as he reached under his smock, unfastened his breast pocket and removed a joint. There were NO SMOKING signs posted all over the basement, but Kevin ignored them. He'd been performing this little ritual ever since he'd gotten the job and had found a way to keep the smell from lingering.

Near the ceiling was a rectangular window about two feet by three with a sturdy padlock on a hinge-latch. Months ago, Kevin had tried every small key on the ring that hung in the kitchen until the lock chittered free.

Now he climbed a couple crates and unlocked the window, pulling it open to let in a blast of icy air. He sat on the crate, cupped his hand around the lighter and lit the joint, drawing the sweet smoke in deeply and holding it in his lungs.

His job was the best thing that had happened to him in a long time. Aside from being around Jenny—something he enjoyed so much that he figured it was probably weird... unhealthy, or something—it got him out of the house and away from the constant screaming that was a way of life for his uncle Mike and aunt Sylvia. He'd been living with them since his parents were killed in a house fire almost four years ago and he'd hated every minute of it. Most of the time they seemed unaware of his presence and when they did notice him, it was only to shout at him for one thing or another. His parents hadn't been much better, but at least they weren't screaming all the time and they didn't live in Yreka. He'd tried saving money with the hope of moving south to Redding on his own when he could afford it, but jobs didn't pay much in Yreka and he wasn't going to get any help from Mike and Sylvia, so he held his money in an iron grip. His only luxury was the little baggy of marijuana he bought every couple months from Corky Potter who lived, appropriately, in nearby Weed. He hadn't been on a date in all the years he'd lived in Yreka and he didn't go to movies or eat out; he had no friends to speak of, but that was okay because, the way he saw it, having friends meant having to spend money now and then, so he couldn't afford them. He had his job, and he enjoyed it.

After the second hit, Kevin began to feel the effects of the grass—a little relaxed, a little horny—but decided he had time for one more hit before getting the cheese and going back upstairs. He inhaled a third time and lifted his face to the window so the smoke would waft outside and—

—a small white face smiled at him from outside and said, "Smells good."

Kevin fell from the crate and landed on the cement with an explosive grunt. He scrambled to his feet coughing and spun around as two legs slid through the open window.

"Sorry," the girl said, still smiling as she hopped off the crates. "Didn't mean to scare you." She brushed snow from her curly brown hair and the shoulders of her blue down jacket. "Are you okay?"

Kevin was shaken, but unhurt. "Y-yeah, I'm fine, but… um, you shouldn't be in here. I could get into trouble."

"I think you could get into trouble all by yourself." She looked down at the smoldering joint on the floor.

Kevin stamped out the ember with the toe of his shoe and put the joint back in his pocket. "Yeah, well… you should go." He fidgeted, looking the girl up and down quickly, then turning toward the freezer.

"Why? Is somebody else coming down here?"

"Maybe," he lied, opening the freezer.

"Ah. You're expecting company? Your girlfriend, maybe?"

He heard her footsteps on the concrete as she followed him. He said nothing as he searched for the boxes of shredded cheese.

"You have a girlfriend?"

He hefted the box out of the freezer, looking at the girl again. She was kind of cute. No… cute wasn't exactly the right word. Exotic…yes, she was exotic. She had very pretty dark eyes, heavy lidded, as if she were sleepy, and smooth lips which she licked as she unzipped her puffy jacket.

"Look, I'm working right now, okay?" He tried to sound firm but he was preoccupied with the open front of her jacket, with the impressive curve of her breasts beneath the black sweatshirt she wore, and with the tingly feeling that had already been stirred in him by the marijuana. He put the box down and added, "I've been down here too long already."

"Oh. So you aren't waiting for your girlfriend."

"No. Um, you've gotta go now. Really." He was sounding less convincing each time he spoke.

"Out there? But it's so cold."

"Go inside. Get some coffee."

"It's packed in there. Besides, I don't have any money. I'm stuck here." She slipped her jacket off and tossed it onto the crate behind her. On her sweatshirt, red letters stretched taut over her surprisingly large breasts: EASY BUT NOT CHEAP.

He thought about it a long time. Yes, he could get into trouble. But no one ever came down to the basement besides Kevin and he did have a break coming. He could even take it early.

"So you want to stay down here a while?" he asked.

Her eyes brightened a little. "Could I? I promise not to touch anything and I won't make any noise. I'll just sit down here for a while, that's all. I could use the rest."

The marijuana was making him feel a little more sure of himself than he would have been otherwise and he nodded slowly as he looked the girl over. What skin he could see looked silky; she wore no bra and when she moved, her breasts shifted slightly beneath the black material. She was probably seventeen, maybe eighteen. Yes...exotic. In spite of his boldness—he usually found it difficult to stare so shamelessly at women—he was nervous inside, jittery, and his mouth felt dry. The condition worsened as he let his mind wander through the possibilities.

Kevin had never been with a girl before, never touched a girl. He was too busy saving his money to spend it on dinners and movies and whatever else people did on dates. But this would be different. This would be free.

"Okay," he said, going back into the freezer. He got the second box of cheese, brought it out and put it on top of the first and pushed the freezer door shut.

"I can stay, you mean?"

"Yeah."

"Oh, jeez, thanks, I really—"

She stopped when he stepped in front of her and, trying hard to bury his nervousness, said, "But what do I get for letting you?"

She stared at him expressionlessly a moment, then smirked again. Her tongue flicked out over her lower lip, there and gone in a flash, like a snake's. "Well…" She looked him over then held his eyes with hers. "What do you want?"

"I let you stay here and I get to… spend my break with you."

"Okay. Yeah." She lifted a hand and brushed her fingertips lightly over his throat just below his jaw. Kevin almost flinched, but resisted. "Yeah, you come back."

As he lifted the boxes and started upstairs, Kevin felt her watching him, felt those heavy lidded eyes on his back. Half way up, he turned and looked down at her.

She was watching him, sitting on her coat on the crate, legs spread; her elbows rested on her knees, arms dangling between her thighs, long fingers twitching. She was smiling.

"I'll leave the light on," he said.

"No, that's okay." It was nearly a whisper. "I like the dark."

As Kevin started back up the stairs, she added, "Take your break early."

His thoughts were so concentrated on the girl that he completely forgot to relock the window. In fact, he was so preoccupied that, later, as he hurried from table to table in the restaurant, he didn't even realize that he was ignoring Jenny completely, as if she weren't even there…

CHAPTER 8

Jon watched his dad grow smaller.

As he told Jon about the night he'd taken a sickly girl into his sleeper in Missouri, about the black truck she'd gotten into and the man who'd driven it away, Dad hunched farther and farther forward until he seemed to be curling into a ball behind the wheel. After a long pause, he continued:

"After that, when I realized this was not going to go away, when I realized what I was, I—"

"What do you mean, what you are? What're you—"

"Just let me finish, Jon. I made arrangements for the divorce right away and let your mother have everything. Well, almost everything. I had my lawyer wire me some money from my savings account, enough to live on for a while." He seemed to think about that a moment, then chuckled coldly, muttering, "Enough to live on. Hmph. Anyway, I left her everything else. I knew I wouldn't need it. I sure wasn't going to go home. I didn't want to expose any of you to this...to me. I still didn't understand it and didn't know how to handle it. But I knew I was different. I noticed changes in myself, weird changes, in the next couple of days. Like, breathing...I caught myself not breathing sometimes, just not taking in any breath. I realized I could go for hours without a single breath. Now, I have to make a conscious effort to breathe. It just doesn't come naturally. And sunlight. I couldn't stand the sunlight, Jonny, still can't. And when I tried to eat food or drink anything, even water? I got sick, deathly ill. But I still felt hungry, I craved...something. I got bad...weak, shaky, cold. I finally stopped one night at a hospital in Kansas and went into the emergency room. There was a boy there. He'd been hit by a car and they were just taking him in. He'd bled a lot. All over the waiting room. It was on the floor, one of the sofas. I could smell it the second I walked in and I just went...crazy. I dropped to my knees and put my face down on the floor and just started licking it up. Rubbed my face all around in it like some animal. The receptionist started screaming and a doctor ran out and just... stood there. Looking at me. Like he couldn't believe what he was seeing. Hell, I couldn't believe what I was doing. But it was good, it was so good. And I felt better. Stronger. More alert. After a few seconds, the doctor came for me, shouting something. I'm not sure what. I hauled ass out of there, ran to my truck and took off. But I knew for sure what I was then. And what I needed. And I knew I needed more of it right away. Now...I couldn't believe it at first, even after I knew. It was happening to me and I couldn't believe it, because it was just too...too crazy. But it was true. And I was hungry." He wiped his face with a palm and turned away from Jon, silent for a while.

Jon felt a chill inside his chest, as if his lungs had frozen. He realized his fists were clenched in his lap and his entire body was tense. He was afraid he might get sick. He decided that was understandable under the circumstances. After sixteen years of looking up to his dad, a good man, a strong, warm and solid man, he was now having to adjust to the fact that his dad had completely lost his mind. His dad was insane.

"There was a hitchhiker," Dad went on quietly. "A girl. Young. I picked her up. I... hurt her. But I didn't kill her. I don't think I did, anyway. I tried hard just to take what I needed, then I left her beside the road. Unconscious."

Jon had to swallow a lump of nausea in his throat before he spoke: "God, Dad, you, I mean, do you hear what you're—"

"But I haven't done it again" he added quickly. "And I won't. I get it in other ways. I don't want to hurt anyone. So I... I take it from animals. Or I steal it. From a hospital or a blood bank. But not people, Jonny. I won't hurt anymore people." Bill rubbed his eyes wearily with one hand and massaged the back of his neck with another before he continued. "But lately... well, I haven't been feeling too well, lately. Not sure what's wrong, either. Just feels sorta like...like I've got a bad case of the flu all the time.

Or worse, maybe. I don't know." He shook his head as his voice faded into a whisper.

Tears spilled down Jon's cheeks. He started to reach for his dad's hand but pulled back, unable to touch him. His voice was thick when he spoke: "Dad, you...you've gotta see a doctor. Really. Right away. There's gotta be a, a, a hospital here, right? Somewhere close, right? We could take you into emer—"

"A doctor can't help me, Jon. Do you know what they would do if they found out what I am? Do you know?"

"Dad, you don't know that... Dad, there's no—" He had to stop, take a breath. "Listen to yourself, Dad. Remember when I was a little kid and you'd let me watch Creature Features even though you knew you'd be up all night telling me it was just a movie, that there was no such thing as ghosts and monsters and...Dad, you...you need help." He turned away quickly, ashamed of what he'd said and not wanting his dad to see him crying. He felt cold fingers on his chin, felt his dad turn his face around until they were looking at one another again. Jon tried to pull away, couldn't bare to see him, to see what had happened to his eyes and face, but Dad's grip was strong.

"Look at me," Dad said. "Jonny. Look at me, Jon. Look!"

Jon wiped a tear from his eye and looked at his dad. Watched him as he opened his mouth slowly, opened it farther and farther. He saw something move in Dad's mouth, two somethings, lowering in his mouth, extending downward. Two teeth. Incisors. Growing as his mouth opened. Sliding from his gum like a snake's fangs. Needle points glistening with saliva.

Jon began to cry like a baby.

Bill was quick to calm his son down, holding him and assuring him there was nothing to be afraid of; though at first Jon struggled and refused to listen, he returned Bill's embrace after a few moments and begged him to see a doctor, to get help, to do something about whatever disease had done this to him. Bill said again that, although he still did not fully understand his condition, he was certain a doctor could do nothing.

They talked a while longer and Bill tried to change the subject; Jon told him more about Grandma's stroke and the wreck they had and Bill asked him about the girls, about his friends back home and, of course, about A.J.—Bill's pet name for Adelle Janine—whom he was sure was somewhere in the truck stop at that moment, worried about Jon, wondering where he was and, considering their chilly relationship, wondering if he'd perhaps just left, caught a ride with someone and taken off.

"You've got to go back inside, Jon."

"Come with me."

The words made Bill ache. "I can't," he whispered. "You know that."

"Then let me stay with you!"

He simply shook his head, unable to speak for a moment. Then: "C'mon, I'll walk you. There're a few more things I want to tell you."

Outside, their feet crunching through the crusty snow beside the road, Bill said, "You've got to promise me something, Jonny. You can't tell your mother you saw me. No matter what."

The boy said nothing, but seemed to understand, to know the kind of trouble that would cause; or maybe he didn't speak because he'd had the wind knocked out of him by it all and was still stunned into silence.

"Can I see you again later?" he asked after a bit. "We're gonna be here a while, you know. Probably all night. I could come out after I eat, tell Mom I'm gonna play video games or go look around or something and come out—"

"No. No, Jon, don't go outside. Listen to me." They stopped in the middle of the parking lot and faced one another in the falling snow. "Remember the girl I told you about? The girl who bit me? And the man who drove the truck?"

He nodded.

"They're here. Tonight. In fact, there are two trucks. That's why I'm here. To find them."

"Whuh…what're you gonna do?"

"Well, I'm…not sure yet. But if they did this to me, then they've done it to others. And will probably do it to more. I've been following them. It hasn't been easy because I can't start driving until dusk and have to stop at dawn. They drive during the day. Which means the driver isn't…he's not like me. Like them."

Something changed in the boy's face; his eyes narrowed and his lower lip tucked between his teeth slightly. It was a thoughtful, scheming look. "What'd you say he looked like?"

Firmly: "You listen to me, Jonathan, you just stay with your mother. Don't even think about it, you hear me? Stay out of it."

"You said he was fat and ugly and smelled bad."

"Goddammit, boy, I'm still your dad and I'll whip your—"

"Does he have really bad teeth?"

Bill's tongue froze mid-sentence and he stared at his son, then nodded slowly.

"He's inside. I saw him. With another guy. They came in right behind us and the first guy was talking real loud about this bloody mess in the store."

"Bloody mess?"

"There was a fight and some guy bashed in another guy's nose. There was blood all over the floor and this fat smelly guy saw it and said to his friend to…to, um…" He clenched his eyes and thought hard, "…he said something like, 'Go make sure they don't come in here 'cause this'll drive 'em crazy,' something like that."

Bill moved closer to him, suddenly tense. "Did you see them again? Where did they go?"

"No. I don't know. I came out here right after we got a table because—" He froze, jaw slack.

"What? Because why?"

Jon told him of the girl he'd seen outside the window, the girl with the big eyes and pale skin who had disappeared so quickly.

Bill clutched Jon's shoulders and said, "You listen to me, boy. See my face? See my skin? While you're here, you don't go anywhere near anyone who looks like me, man or woman. You steer clear of anybody who looks sick or even a little suspicious, you hear me?" He was squeezing Jon's shoulders tightly, shaking him a little.

Jon's eyes widened a little fearfully as he nodded.

"And don't go off by yourself. Stay with your mother and… what's his name? Her boyfriend?"

"Doug."

"Yeah. You stay with them. And keep an eye on your sisters."

"I'm…not gonna see you again?"

Bill wrapped his arms around his son and whispered, "I'll be here. I'll be watching you. I won't be far away. You…yeah, you might see me again," he lied. He didn't want that. Never again. It hurt too much. "You might. Now. Get back inside and apologize to your mom for running off." He slapped Jon's back, turned him toward the building and gave him a little shove.

In the distance, a siren mourned.

After a few steps, Jon turned back.

"Go on. Get some dinner. The food's good here, remember?"

Jon nodded, then hurried inside with his head down.

Bill watched him disappear in the crowded foyer, then relaxed, no longer trying to hide the heaviness he felt; his shoulders slumped and he teetered a bit on his feet, stumbling to maintain his balance.

He headed toward the restaurant's windows, weaving between the cars, staying in the shadows. Within weeks of contracting his illness—that was how he thought of it, an "illness," because with it came things that he feared would get out of control, or take control, if he thought of it in anything approaching positive terms—he'd discovered his ability to remain unseen. Darkness had become his natural element and he was drawn to it like a shark to deep waters; in shadow, he became a shadow, and moved with more agility without so much as a breath or a blink to betray his presence. He found the shadows now, followed them without a thought, moving through them as smoothly as blood through an artery, until he was standing just a couple feet from the first window.

Pulsing red and blue light from behind made Bill spin around; a police car was pulling into the parking lot. Probably because of the fight, he thought, turning to the window again. When he spotted Jon inside, weaving through the crowd, Bill followed him, moving fluidly through the shadows, until Jon reached their booth by the window.

And there they were. A.J. and Dara and Cece and…Doug. Bill wondered how they'd met and, although he'd never seen him before, he wondered if A.J. had known Doug before she and Bill split up. If she'd known him well... if maybe Doug had been her reason for not coming back to Bill the last time...

Jon started to scoot in beside Cece and Doug and—

—he stopped. His eyes were locked on something behind A.J. His lips were parted and he was stooped forward, frozen in a half-sitting position.

Bill followed his gaze to the next booth where two fat ugly men sat eating sloppily, chewing with their mouths open, food clinging to their lips.

The Carsey Brothers...

CHAPTER 9

When Byron looked out the window and saw the police car drive up, he thought immediately of David and headed toward the rear exit.

David Pike worked on the gas island, a nice enough kid, twenty-one or -two, with a thin beard that failed to cover the scattered pocks left over from high school acne. Byron liked him and they sometimes had coffee on their break. But only when David wasn't off with some girl, usually one of the lot lizards, which, of course, was a strictly forbidden activity for the employees and which, because he thought David was an okay guy, concerned Byron. David had a problem holding down jobs—which was understandable considering his preoccupation with anything in a skirt—and Byron was afraid he'd be losing this one soon if he wasn't more careful.

About twenty minutes ago or so, Byron had been mopping the floor in front of the fuel desk and had looked out the window to see David talking with a young girl by the gas tanks. She didn't appear to be buying gas and, judging by their posture and the way David was smiling, she wasn't asking directions either. And Byron had seen enough lot lizards come and go in the truck stop—scruffy, haggard girls, usually gaunt and frail looking—to know this girl wasn't just looking for a nice word and a smile. At the time, he'd continued mopping, clicking his tongue and shaking his head, hoping the boy didn't push his luck too far.

Then, as he was cleaning up a spilled Coke in the travel store, he saw the police car and thought of David again. The cop was no doubt coming in response to the call regarding the man who'd been attacked with a flashlight earlier, but there was always the chance he might stroll out back and take a look around after that was cleared up.

Peering out the window opposite the fuel desk, Byron couldn't see David. He clicked his tongue again, shook his head again and said to one of the girls behind the desk, "Lynda, I'm gonna be outside for just a second in case somebody wants me, okay?"

She nodded and Byron passed the bank of payphones, leaning his mop against the wall, and went outside, shivering as he stepped into the cold snowy night. Lee Russell, a pot bellied fellow with a bulbous nose that gave away all the drinking he did on his days off, was making change for a customer who had just filled up.

"Hey, Lee!" Byron called.

He looked over his shoulder and nodded in acknowledgement.

"Where's David?"

"I dunno, he took an early break, can you believe that? Again!" To the customer, an older man in an overcoat and fedora: "You have a good night now. But if I was you, I'd sit it out for a while."

The man shook his head, jingling his car keys; he looked grumpy. "No, I'm going to turn around and head back. Just wasting time here."

Lee shrugged and said, "Suit yourself." Then to Byron again: "He went out toward the shop, I think." Holding his elbows close to his sides, extending his forearms and doubling both fists, Lee thrust his pelvis forward a couple times and said, "Know what I mean?"

Byron nodded; he knew. And he knew exactly where to find David. There was a small cement-floored room behind the shop with a table, chairs, a rickety sofa, an old black and white rabbit-eared television and a refrigerator. Sometimes when business was slow, the guys would go back there and play cards, drink Cokes and smoke a lot. That was where David always went when he wanted a little privacy with one of the lizards, and Byron was sure he was there now, probably on the sofa with his pants down around his ankles.

Byron headed that way, pulling out his key ring and finding

the key that would open that back room, because he knew David would have it locked. Going through the shop, Byron passed Buddy Pritchard, one of the mechanics, hunching under the hood of a Mack. "David come through here?" he asked.

"Yup. In the back. But I don't think he wants anymore company," the mechanic chuckled, never turning away from his work.

Without pausing, Byron went to the door in the dark narrow corridor in back and slipped the key in, opening it without knocking. He figured maybe a surprise visit would shake the boy up a little, make him think twice next time.

"David?" he said, stepping inside. "We got a cop out fruh—"

The only light came from a small covered lamp on the card table. David sat on the sofa with his head leaning back and arms limp at his sides. His pants were around his ankles, just as Byron had expected, and the girl he'd seen through the window earlier was kneeling between David's legs, slurping.

But something was wrong.

David was panting. His chest was heaving up and down in rapid piston-like rhythm and his mouth and eyes were open wide. Too wide. Not the kind of a wide that comes with pleasure but with fear or pain. And the girl, who didn't react to Byron's presence for a moment, held David's cock in her fist, pounding frantically, holding it to the side so it was out of the way of her face, which was buried in the fold of flesh between David's thigh and groin. Her head moved up and down, back and forth, and the noise she made…such a loud, thick sound, like a calf sucking its mother's tit.

And David continued to pant, unaware of Byron. He looked so pale in the poor light.

Feeling bad now, regretting the intrusion, Byron repeated, "David, there's a cop out—"

The girl spun around, dark hair flying about her face with the sudden movement.

Something dribbled from her mouth. Something dark.

It was on David's leg, too, smeared there like jam on toast.

David kept panting…panting and panting…

Byron said quietly, "What in theee fuck—"

The girl dove. She shot across the room like an attacking dog, bloody hands outstretched, mouth yawning open and eyes narrowed to black cuts. And something else, something impossible, something ridiculous. She had—

—fangs. They were long and curved and red with David's blood and they seemed to grow longer as her lips pulled back and her mouth opened wider. She hissed—an awful sound, colder than the snow outside—and her palms struck Byron's chest and slammed him back against a four foot high bookshelf full of grimy thick binders, grease stained telephone books and catalogs, and his lungs emptied under the force of her blow. He slid to the floor and fell on his side in front of the open door, clutching his chest and fighting for a breath, just one breath, but his lungs did not seem to be there anymore and—

—the girl closed her fists around his shirt and—

—No, Byron thought as his scalp shriveled, no, she can't do this, she's too tiny, just a tiny little thing, just a kid, she can't, she just can't, SHE CAN'T BE FUCKIN' DOIN' THIS!—

—she lifted him off the cement floor, his whole body, all two hundred and sixty pounds of him, just swept him up and threw him across the room, and—

—Byron hit the back of the sofa with a monstrous thud, pounding the whole sofa against the wall, then he rolled to the floor at David's feet. He was getting up instantly, rising to his knees and turning toward the door, but—

—the girl was gone.

Gagging as he tried to breathe, Byron half-crawled to the door, leaning against the doorjamb as he pulled himself to his feet and leaned out to look down the corridor and into the shop.

Buddy was still working on the truck. The girl was not there.

Byron tried to speak several times before he actually made a sound and when he did, his voice was like rusty pipes: "Stuh-stop that guh-girl! Stop 'er!"

Buddy looked at Byron distractedly. "Huh? What?"

"That guh-girl!" He pointed with a shaking hand. "Just ran through here. Stop her!"

"What girl?"

"The one who—she just ran—she was just—"

"Nobody's been through here but you." Annoyed, he went back to work, muttering, "The hell you guys doin' in there, anyways?"

Byron spun around, nearly falling, and staggered across the room to David's side.

His eyes and mouth were still open wide, but he'd stopped panting. In fact, he looked like he'd stopped breathing. His erection twitched, smeared with blood; his dark pubic hairs were caked with it, matted and glistening, and more of it ran from the wound beside his groin.

Byron fell onto the sofa and slapped a hand onto David's chest, shaking him as he barked, "David! David, are you okay?"

The young man blinked, lifted his head slowly, lips curling into a drunken smile. When he saw Byron, the smile disappeared and he blinked some more, rapidly, confused. "Whatreyou..." He looked around, frowning. "Where'd she go? She wasn't even—she didn' fin—"

He saw the blood. Stared at it the way he might have stared at a tap dancing frog. Then he screamed, "Jesus Gawd Jesus Gawd I'm bleeding I'm bleeding Jesus Gawd Jesus Gaw—"

Byron gripped his shoulders and pushed him back, squeezing as he said, "S'okay, Dave, s'okay, now, you're gonna be fine, just fine, so calm down, now, calm down." Then, over his shoulder, he shouted, "Get some help!"

Buddy came to the door and stared for a long moment, wiping his hands on a dirty rag. "The hell happened here?"

"Goddammit, just get some help!" In the small space, Byron's tremendous voice sounded as if it could move furniture and Buddy flinched, then hurried away. Turning to David, he asked softly, "What happened, now, David? Tell me. What'd she do?"

He'd stopped screaming and was whimpering now, head shaking back and forth, back and forth as he said, again and again, "Not bad, please God, don't let it be bad, not bad, not too bad..."

There was a large metal sink in the corner of the room with a paper towel dispenser above it on the wall. Byron got a towel, wet it, and knelt beside David, dabbing the blood away gently.

David had stopped looking down.

There were two wounds—puncture marks—and not very neat ones.

Byron pressed the wet towel over the wounds and tried to stop the bleeding, thinking all the while of the girl. Her teeth. No, no...fangs, he reminded himself, blowing hard through pursed lips and puffing his cheeks.

"She bit me, Byron," David rasped, clutching Byron's sleeve. His face was colorless and his saucered eyes were watering. "And I knew it. I knew it."

"You knew what?"

"I knew what she was doing, but...but I couldn't, you know... stop her because it...it felt good. I thought she was gonna suck me off but she bit me and, Goddamn, Byron, it felt good!"

He stared up at Byron with the expression of a man who has just realized that everything he's ever been taught in his whole life thus far is wrong; for a moment, his grip on Byron's sleeve tightened, then his whole body became limp and his head fell back, mouth open. He made more whimpering sounds— "Ooohh-ho, oh-ho boy, ooohh..."—then said, "I don't feel so good, Byron."

"Yeah, I know, buddy, but you're gonna be fine. Somebody's coming." He stared at David's deadly pale complexion, noticed the way his skin seemed to sag as if he'd lost even the slightest muscle tone. A simple bite would not have done that. But Byron knew it had not been a simple bite.

He remembered the awful slurping sounds he'd heard upon entering the room...

"Well," Byron said, trying to sound jovial, "maybe this'll teach you. No more screwing around on the job." He chuckled and patted David's shoulder. But he was not jovial and the chuckle and gesture were lies. He was worried. That girl, whoever she was, had sucked blood from David Pike's crotch and now she was out there somewhere.

Worst of all, Byron could not—no matter how hard he tried— remember what she looked like. And something told him that David wouldn't remember either...

CHAPTER 10

About twenty minutes before Byron discovered David in the shop's back room, a terrible accident occurred on Interstate 5 between the Sierra Gold Pan Truck Stop and Yreka. It was the kind of accident that no one involved saw coming, not even in the final two seconds before it actually happened, and which no one involved could explain later. It just happened.

Eight vehicles were involved.

Three of the vehicles were eighteen wheelers, two of which were tankers, and their trailers were scattered like seeds in a new garden. The trailers, once they came to rest, managed to block Interstate 5 in both directions, the tanks spilling their contents onto the highway.

This was the news that Deputy Travis Cody of the Yreka Sheriff's Office brought with him when he arrived at the Sierra Gold Pan Truck Stop in response to a call regarding a parking lot fight. In the office of the truck stop's travel store, Cody shared the news hurriedly with the injured man, one Malcolm Osick, and one of the store's cashiers, Bette Fremon.

"I'm really sorry," Cody said, "but you're gonna be cut off from the hospital for a long time because of the chemical spill and I gotta get over to the scene right now, so you'll have to do the best you can until I can get somebody over here or come back for you myself."

Osick lay groaning on a cot and Bette sat beside him, an open first aid kit on her lap, dabbing Osick's battered nose with a piece of gauze dipped in alcohol.

Cody was winding up his apology quickly as he backed out of the office when he collided with Buddy Pritchard, who was stumbling into the office looking haggard and a little ill.

"Oh, um, yeah, yeah," Buddy said, running a hand through his wet snowy hair, "Byron said you'd be here. Um, yeah, um, we need you over to the shop. There's a guy there, David, a guy from the gas island. He's, um, bleeding. Really bad. I don't know what's happened, but there's, um, blood. A lotta blood. I think he's hurt pretty bad."

Cody rolled his eyes slowly and sighed, shaking his head. That was when he suggested that Bette get on the P. A. and page a doctor or nurse...

"Where the hell have you been?" Adelle hissed when Jon returned.

Jon started to scoot in beside Dara when Doug saw him freeze, half seated, eyes locked on the space between Doug and Adelle and just above Cece's head. He didn't move for a moment, just stared, suspended in his awkward about-to-sit position. Then he dropped into the seat, blinking rapidly, suddenly looking ashen, drained, as if he'd just seen aliens land in the parking lot.

Jon said quietly, "I was just...um, playing some video games... is all." He bowed his head and frowned at his cheeseburger.

"Well, your food's getting cold," Adelle said, her tone softer now. "C'mon, eat up, hon." She was just now beginning to wind down from her conversation with her sister; Doug could almost see the tension rolling off her like beads of perspiration.

Jon picked up the burger and took a bite hesitantly, as if he weren't sure what rested between the sesame seed buns. As he chewed, his eyes wandered to that space above Cece's head again, staring at something.

Trying to be inconspicuous, Doug looked back over his shoulder. He saw nothing unusual, nothing to warrant the troubled look in Jon's eyes. There was just the crowded restaurant and, seated in the next booth, the two loud unbathed men Doug had seen out front earlier; the worst of the two faced Doug and both were hunched over their plates eating noisily and sloppily.

"You feeling okay, Jon?" Doug asked.

He jerked as if startled by the question and said, "Yeah.

Yeah, I'm fine." He turned his gaze to the window and peered between the open blinds. As he ate, his eyes darted back and forth between the window and that space behind Doug, as if there were something back there distracting him, tugging at his attention.

Doug decided it was the wreck; what had happened—what might have happened—was probably just now hitting Jon. It had struck Doug earlier; he'd been standing at a payphone thumbing through the Yellow Pages in search of an all night towing service and garage when he'd realized, quite suddenly, as if it hadn't occurred to him before, that they'd had a car accident and that they could have been terribly hurt, even killed...all of them. The thought made his scalp tingle.

After two calls, Doug realized that there was no chance they'd get the car towed before daylight, let alone get back on the road by then. No one, in fact, was going anywhere. The freeways were closing, the lights in the truck stop were flickering and the snow was falling harder than ever, so hard that the plow couldn't keep up with it and the parking lot was getting buried in the white powder. He'd finally given up and replaced the receiver with a long weary sigh, hoping Adelle's mother could hang on until they got there...whenever that would be.

They ate in silence for a while. The girls' concentration was focused entirely on their food while Adelle ate slowly and thoughtfully; Jon, on the other hand, continued his mysterious staring. It was so annoying that Doug even looked over his shoulder a couple more times, expecting to see something interesting. Finally, he asked, "Jon, what are you staring at?"

"Staring? Nothing. Nothing. I'm not staring." Jon's response was quick and breathy, trembling with guilt, and Jon was about to pursue the question when a timid female voice spoke over the P.A. system:

"Your attention, please? Your attention? We're sorry for the interruption, but... if there are any doctors or nurses dining in the restaurant, could you please come to the register? We have two injured men who are in need of attention. If any medical personnel are dining in the restaurant could you please come to the register, we'd really appreciate it."

Adelle sighed and put down her fork, glancing at Doug.

"C'mon, honey, you're tired," Doug said. "Let someone else—"

"That could've been us, you know," she said quietly. "We got off lucky tonight." She looked around to see if anyone else was getting up. A short, well dressed middle-aged man was leaving his table and heading for the front, dabbing his mouth with a napkin. Patting Cece's knee, she said, "Let me out, hon. I'll be back in a while."

"Want me to come?" Doug asked.

She smiled tiredly and shook her head. "I doubt they'll need X-rays."

As Doug slid back into the booth, he said, "It's probably nothing serious. Probably just a—" He stopped and stared across the table.

Jon's cheeseburger lay scattered on his plate where he'd dropped it; a piece of lettuce hung from his lips and his face had lost all color as he stared open-mouthed after his mother.

"Jon, what's the matter?"

"What...what do you think...happened?"

"Oh, it's probably nothing. Remember that guy we saw when we came in? The guy who was bleeding? Probably him. Probably a couple guys knocked each other around, is all."

Adelle returned to the table and leaned over Doug. "I need my coat," she said. "One of the guys is outside."

As she walked away, Jon wiped his mouth quickly on his napkin and stood.

"What're you doing?" Doug asked.

"Going with her."

"No, you shouldn't—"

But he was gone.

"He is so gross," Dara sneered. "He gets off on seeing people bleed."

"Well, girls," Doug said, "I guess it's just us." He started twirling his fork in his spaghetti, but his fingers slowed down a bit and he cocked his head to one side when he heard urgent, hissing whispers from the booth behind him.

"—whatta you think? What would happen then, huh?"

"It coulda been anything! A heart attack, a-a-a, I don't know, a kid with a bloody nose!"

"I don't care what it coulda been. Get off your ass and check it out."

A utensil clattered angrily against a plate. "How come I gotta do all this shit? I'm haulin' the fuckin' queen!"

"Whatsat give you, seniority? You think that's some kinda privilege? You're haulin' that fuckin' thing because I don't wanna get near it. Now get out there, Goddammit!" Keys jangled noisily. "An' here. Take these and get my cigars outta my truck."

Doug felt the back of his seat shift as the man sitting directly behind him got up.

There was something odd about those two men, something beneath their soiled, lumpy exteriors that was equally repulsive. Doug jerked his head from side to side once, as if shooing a fly, and continued eating his spaghetti.

As he followed the small group through the shop at a distance, Jon heard the short man introduce himself as Dr. Phillip Kane. Jon's mother walked beside the doctor hurriedly, led by the woman from the travel store and one of the mechanics. They went down a narrow corridor at the back of the shop and through a doorway. Jon slowed his pace and approached the door cautiously, not wanting to be seen.

All four of them joined a police officer and the janitor from the restaurant and hunched over a man on a sofa. There was a great deal of blood on the man's bare legs.

"Good God!" the doctor snapped. "This man's lost a lot of blood!"

"Yeah, that's obvious," Deputy Cody murmured.

"No," Dr. Kane said, "more. I mean more blood than there is here. Was he stabbed? Did you bring him here? Was he—"

"Somebody bit him," the black man said.

"Bit him? You're kidding?" To the man on the sofa, the doctor said, "Sir? I'm a doctor. Could you tell me what happened? Sir?"

The man simply groaned.

After watching for a few more minutes, Jon turned and went

back down the corridor, through the shop and out into the cold. He jogged to the corner of the main building and leaned against the wall. It was more than just the temperature that made him shiver. He knew what was wrong with the bleeding man in that small dark room, but no one would believe him if he told them.

No one but his dad…

She smiled in the dark of the basement beneath the restaurant's kitchen, sitting on a crate, hugging her knees to her chest. Her name was Amy.

Things were working out much better than she'd expected.

Months ago, she'd decided it was time to break away. The problem was how. She couldn't do it alone. She needed someone to watch over her during the daylight hours, someone to protect her while she slept. But she wanted someone…nice. Someone besides that hideous slob who drove the truck. He smelled, and not just of body odor; his obese body reeked of ill health and decay. But worse than him was the creature that rode in the other truck, the thing that called itself her master, the monster that had made her what she was and now claimed ownership of her soul. The others feared her, would never think of trying to escape her. But Amy was different than the others. She'd always been different than the others.

Amy had been fleeing people who claimed ownership of her long before she'd been bled. She'd fled her cold, affluent parents when she was thirteen; her father's business and her mother's social life had left no time in their lives for Amy. She'd remained a stranger to them no matter how hard she fought for their attention and love; their money, belongings and friends always came first. Since she was a little girl, Amy had had a gnawing fear that she would grow up to be like them, and nothing frightened her more. She'd decided, finally, to leave the luxurious surroundings with which they'd provided her just to keep from catching whatever disease of the soul had made them so empty, so ultimately lifeless. Even now, she reminded herself often that she would not allow herself to become like them. She'd fled an abusive boyfriend who'd threatened to kill her if she ever tried to leave; and she'd escaped the law when she was nailed for prostitution at the age of fifteen.

Now she planned to flee the thing that stayed in the cool darkness of that trailer. She'd seen it only a few times, but once was more than enough. Although she could not change what had been done to her, what she had already become, she was determined—just as she had been with her parents—not to become like that creature. Perhaps it had lived so long—centuries, maybe thousands of years—that it had simply stopped resembling the human it had once been...if it had ever been human. If Amy was doomed to live as long, she would not follow suit. She'd avoided becoming the walking mannequins that were her parents; she would avoid becoming like the monster that never left its dark shelter.

It was true, the Queen did have a powerful hold on her, a psychic grip that would be difficult to break. Her invisible presence never left Amy, never allowed her to feel alone. But she was certain the hold could be broken. With distance. Distance was her goal.

And Kevin was going to help her reach it.

"Not me," she whispered to herself, as she often did, eyes closed as if she were praying. "Not me. I'll never become like that. Not me."

But her eyes snapped open wide suddenly and she stared into the dark trying not to shudder.

She felt the Queen's presence within her. As always when she voiced her planned independence, Amy could feel that presence laughing...

CHAPTER 11

The snowfall had become almost as thick as fog and the back lot was a shadowy forest of long silent trucks with darkened lights and snow covered hoods. Bill wandered between them cautiously, following the shadows with the silence of a cat, blending into the darkness whenever someone walked by. He'd heard the man's scream coming from the shop and considered investigating, but thought better of it; others would be there in seconds and he didn't want to be seen. If it was what he thought it was—and he had little doubt—there was nothing he could do about it now; this was more important.

He found the black Carsey Bros, trucks easily. He walked the length of the nearest one slowly, running his palms lightly along the side, head cocked, listening. There were no sounds inside, not so much as a breath. The trailer was empty. He moved toward the next one, stopping three feet away.

Something in his gut twisted and, for a long moment, he couldn't breathe.

Staring at the side of the trailer, Bill sensed—knew—that he was being watched. No...not watched: observed. And not with eyes...

Something on the other side of the trailer's long white wall was aware of him, tracking him, sizing him up. A solitary something, alone in the trailer's darkness, still and silent. Something he could almost see with his mind's eye, with the senses newly awakened in him, senses he'd been discovering slowly over the past months...

Footsteps.

Bill tensed but could not move, held for a moment in the invisible grip of whatever hunkered inside the trailer.

The footsteps drew nearer and Bill stepped back into darkness, became invisible.

"Some kinda bullshit," a gravelly voice mumbled as a short fat man walked into view, kicking slush with his boots.

Bill inclined his head forward and sniffed the air delicately. The man smelled dirty.

He walked between the black trucks and stopped, facing the first one Bill had approached. He knocked three times on the trailer—one…two-three—then waited. Silence. Then he turned to the other trailer, lifted his hand, knuckle crooked, and—

—he froze. His raised hand trembled and he licked his dry lips anxiously, then repeated the knock. Two knocks responded from inside and the man took a quick step backward, shuddering as he stuffed his hands into his coat pockets. Turning, he walked toward the back of the trailer, muttering, "Goddamned freak, anyways."

Bill backed further into the darkness and watched the man step into the aisle behind the trucks and look in both directions, head bowed against the snow. As the man turned, Bill gathered all his strength—which, even in his weakened condition, would be superior to that of this fat, huffing man—and moved.

The man was face down on the slushy ground between the trailers in a heartbeat with Bill straddling him, clutching his soft round shoulders.

"What the fuh—"

"Shut up," Bill whispered.

"Whattaya want? I ain't got any muh—"

"Just shut up and listen. What's your name?"

"Claude. Carsey."

"You drive one of these trucks?"

"Yuh-yeah. Yeah."

"What are you hauling?"

"Cuh-caskets. Y'know, for dead people. Coffins."

"What was the knocking for?"

"Whuh-whuh-what?"

"You knocked on the trailers. Why?"

"Nunna yer fuckin' bidness."

"Who knocked back? Who's inside the trailer?"

"What the hell d'you—"

Bill got off him, rolled him over and pressed a knee to his chest clutching his collar. When he saw that the man was looking up at him, Bill snapped his mouth open, extending his fangs.

"Oh-oh, sweet Jesus God, no, no, yuh-you're, you're one of 'em," the man whimpered. Bill felt his flabby body quiver beneath him. "Please don't hurt me. Please. I-I swear... I'll...do whatever you want. I swear."

"What do you haul in the trucks?"

The man looked puzzled, confused. "But...you know. Don't you?"

"Tell me."

"Girls. Girls who're...like you. 'Cept they're not in there now. They're working."

"Working?"

"Yeah, the lot. Y'know. Lot lizards? They hook. And then they... well, they get what they need. And they get us what we need. Money. And whatever else they can find."

"Who knocked in there just now?"

The confusion was replaced by fear. The man even seemed to lose some of the color in his face. "You...don't know?" he breathed.

"I'm asking, aren't I?"

"But...you're one of them. How could you not—"

Bill pulled him close until their noses were almost touching. "Don't fuck with me, Claude. Answer my question. Who knocked in the trailer?"

"Buh-but she'll kuh-kill me if I—"

"I've got news for you, Claude. I'm gonna kill you anyway. So just think of this as a final confession. Who is she? What is she? Why is she still in there?"

Claude's eyes darted around and he whispered, as if afraid of being overheard: "We call her their queen. She's like them, but...worse. They're human. Or...they were. Before they... changed. She changed them. And she's not human."

"Why does she stay in the truck?"

"Because she's—" Claude shuddered violently and looked

sick. "—she looks…too different to go out. The girls bring people to her. Usually kids. She likes 'em young. She says they're—" His face twisted briefly. "—fresher."

Bill stared at him for a long moment. He wasn't lying. There were so many questions Bill wanted to ask him, but there was no time; soon, there would be more screams like the one he'd heard earlier. "Does everyone they bite become like them?"

"Nuh-no! God damn, you know what that'd mean? They'd be everywhere! No, they just take what they need and leave 'em. Usually they're unconscious and they wake up later with a little mark somewhere feelin', y'know, hung over."

Anger burned in Bill's chest and he shook the man, growling, "That's a fucking lie! One of them changed me!"

"Really! It's the truth! I don't know what happened to you, but that's the way they do it. Really!"

He still seemed to be telling the truth; he was too terrified to lie. Had the girl told the truth? Had they really broken down and gone for a while without eating? Without feeding? Bill could understand how an overwhelming hunger could make her go too far, take too much.

"Can they be killed?" he asked.

Claude's eyes widened. "Who th'fuck knows? I sure as hell ain't gonna try!"

"Can they be stopped?"

"Wuh-well…they get really sick if they get near garlic. Just—" He cackled nervously. "—just like in the movies."

"How do they—"

"Dad?"

Bill dropped the man to the ground and jerked around with a gasp. Jon stood at the end of one of the trailers, shivering in the cold.

"What the hell are you doing?" Bill hissed. "I told you to stay inside!"

"I couldn't." He told Bill about what he'd heard and seen in the back room of the shop after following Adelle there.

"Well, go back!" Bill snapped. "Now. Get inside."

Jon simply stared at his dad, jaw quaking. "What are you doing, Dad?"

Bill opened his mouth to respond but simply stared at his son silently.

I was just about to kill this man, he thought, that's all.

Jon stared at him with brows furrowed above pained eyes, as if Bill had done something that hurt him. Bill looked down at Claude and saw quivering fear. He closed his eyes, ashamed; suddenly it didn' t matter what Claude Carsey was—an asshole, yes, a monster, definitely, but still a human life—Bill had sworn to himself that he would not kill.

But, aahhh... the temptation...

Bill stood and lifted Claude easily by his collars, slamming him into the side of the trailer. "How do they die?" he growled.

Claude looked as if he were about to cry. "I'm tellin' you, man, I don't know!" he rasped, spittle dribbling over his lumpy lips. "None of 'em've ever died. And that—" He glanced fearfully at the trailer behind Bill and lowered his voice to a breath. "—that thing in there...she's been around for...oh, God, I don't know...she's old, man, I'm tellin' ya. Hundreds a years... maybe thousands, for all I know. I'm tellin' ya...they don't—" He stopped and swallowed hard, his head bobbing; then he hissed, "—you don't die!"

Never loosening his grip, Bill turned to Jon, who had not moved an inch, as if the snow had frozen him where he stood; his eyes had doubled in size and his mouth hung open. "I thought I told you to go inside, boy!" Bill snapped.

Jon shrunk back at the anger in his dad's voice and Bill bit his lip, hating himself for barking at the boy.

"What is it, Jon?" he asked, his voice softer this time.

"A man...in the shop. He's been bitten. I...thought you should know."

Bill nodded. "Yeah. Okay. You go on back inside with your mom, now."

"She's in the shop, too."

In his shock, Bill's grip on Claude's collars loosened. "What?"

"The freeway's closed, so they can't call an ambulance," Jon said. "They called for a doctor or nurse to come help this guy, so Mom went to see if she could do anything."

Bill's arms weakened and almost fell to his sides, but he

pressed his hands to Claude's puffy chest. The thought of A.J. wandering around outside the restaurant horrified him. He whispered, "You mean...your mom is—"

Pain exploded in his groin and shot up into his abdomen like lava from a volcano.

Claude's knee.

His abdomen imploded and all the air left his body.

Claude's fist.

Bill fell to the icy pavement and curled into a groaning ball as Claude's heavy footsteps faded across the lot.

Bill's fingers left trails in the snow as they clawed the ground and he rose slowly with a series of pained grunts. He could still hear Claude puffing as he ran away. Gathering his strength and ignoring his pain, which was fading rapidly anyway—one of the more acceptable changes he'd noticed in himself since being bled—Bill stood, leaning against the trailer.

Jon was at his side, clutching his arm. "Dad! You okay, Dad?"

"Yuh-yeah. Yeah, I'm okay." He looked across the lot and could see Claude weaving his clumsy way between the trucks. He squeezed Jon's shoulder and said, "Stay here, you understand me? Just stay here!"

Bill ran, his feet slapping the snow with a rhythm more than twice as fast as Claude's, but Claude, who was headed for the side entrance to the truck stop, surprised him. The heavy man ducked behind a truck, his feet skittered precariously for a moment and, for a bit, Bill lost him. He could still hear Claude's footsteps, but he couldn't see him, and for a moment wasn't sure in which direction he was headed. Then Bill spotted him.

Claude had doubled back and was heading for the rear of the truck stop; a dark narrow alley ran between the back of the building and the shop and Claude disappeared around a corner.

Bill headed after him again; his pain was completely gone and forgotten now and he was able to run even faster, rounding the back corner and closing the distance between himself and Claude in seconds. He dove for the man's broad back and Claude hit the slushy pavement with a muffled grunt. There was a resounding crack when Claude's forehead slammed into the ground.

Bill rolled the heavy man over with ease and stared into unconscious eyes; the lids were half closed and only glassy whites were visible. A bloody lump was rising quickly on Claude's forehead. When Bill tried to revive him, he got no response, although Claude still had a heartbeat.

"Shit," Bill sighed. He looked back over his shoulder, concerned for Jon's safety; he wanted to milk as much information from Claude as he could, but didn't want to wait around for him to regain consciousness. He looked around frantically, not knowing what he was looking for but spotting something that might be helpful.

To his left there was a small rectangular window level with the ground. Upon closer inspection, he found that it was open a crack. He looked into the darkness inside and saw stacks of boxes and crates and a narrow wooden staircase that led to a door that appeared rather heavy. He only hoped it was kept locked and that no one would come downstairs anytime soon.

Hooking his arms beneath Claude's shoulders, Bill dragged him to the window and, with little effort in spite of his weakness, shoved him headfirst through the window. There was a clatter and a crash, then silence. Bill looked into the window to see Claude lying in a heap on the cement floor surrounded by tumbled boxes and a shattered crate. But once Claude regained consciousness, Bill knew it wouldn't be hard for him to stack some crates back up to the window and climb out. He looked around again.

A filthy garbage dumpster that had once been white stood against the side wall of the shop. Its lid was propped open by the surplus of garbage that rose above the dumpster's lip and hung over the sides.

Bill rolled it across the alley, its wheels screeching with effort, and turned it up on its side directly in front of the window with less than half an inch between the dumpster and the wall. The lid squealed as it swung open and garbage spilled over the ground; the dumpster came to rest with a metallic thump.

Stepping back with his hands on his hips, Bill looked it over to reassure himself that Claude would not be getting out the window…although there was the possibility that he could just wake up and go upstairs.

"What the hell you doing back there?"

Bill spun toward the voice and saw an enormous figure standing at the end of the alley, silhouetted against the lights of the truck lot.

"Huh?" the large man bellowed. It was the voice of a black man, a strong resonant voice. "What're you doing?" He started toward Bill, his big arms held out slightly at his sides as if he were prepared to defend himself. "And what's this mess? What the hell did you do with the damned garbage, man? Huh? Whatta you think you're—"

"Dad!" Jon cried from the lot. "Daaad!"

The man stopped and turned toward the cry.

"That's my son," Bill hissed, rushing past the man, who turned and followed him, growling, "Whole fuckin' place is falling apart tonight..."

Adelle heard Jon's cry, too.

She was leaning over David Pike, who had calmed down in the last few minutes as Adelle and the doctor washed and tended his wound. Deputy Cody had just announced that he couldn't stay any longer when she heard the distant, fearful cry. Adelle froze, listened and heard it again an instant later.

"My God," she breathed.

"Excuse me?" Dr. Kane said, blinking.

She listened. The voice cried out again and there was no doubt in her mind that it was Jon, but...was he calling for his dad?

Adelle shot to her feet, dropping the bloody rag she'd been using to clean Pike's wound, and clutched Deputy Cody's elbow. "My God, that's my son," she said.

Cody looked both puzzled and irritated and started to pull his arm away when he heard the voice, too.

She shook his arm and said firmly, "That's my son, something's wrong with my son," as she started out of the room, pulling Cody with her...

Bill moved fast, weaving around the trucks, much faster than the big man behind him, although the heavy footsteps were trying to keep up.

Stupid, Bill thought, what a stupid, stupid thing to do, leaving him alone like that when you know they're—

He ducked between the two Carsey Bros, trucks and stopped so fast that his feet slid over the icy pavement.

Jon had done as Bill had told him; he'd stayed where Bill had left him. But now he was not alone.

It was dark between the two trucks, but Bill could see its eyes glistening wetly and the long dark nails that extended from its fingers stood out against the pale skin of Jon's throat. Jon's eyes were wide with panic and his chest jackhammered up and down with rapid breaths.

"I could kill him in an instant," it said in a soft, sibilant voice that spoke with the accents of countless languages and seemed slightly garbled, as if there were something in its mouth. Teeth, perhaps. Lots and lots of malformed teeth. "Or I could bleed him. Feed on him. Make him just like you. Would you like that?"

Bill considered rushing the thing, wrestling Jon away from it, but he couldn't take his eyes off that black claw, the tip of which pressed delicately on Jon's throat, puckering the flesh.

…she looks…too different to go out, Claude Carsey had said.

"God, no," Bill whispered. "Don't do that. Please."

Footsteps crunched through the snow, stopping behind Bill, and the big man muttered, "Oh, Lord in heaven."

"Then bring Mr. Carsey back," the voice hissed, like a needle cutting across ice.

"He's…he's okay."

"I don't care about that. Bring him back."

"Lord in heaven," the man said again, repeating it over and over under his breath.

"Give me my son," Bill said, trying to sound firm, authoritative.

The voice laughed. Rather, it was more of an animal-like sound that resembled a laugh than actual human laughter. "What do you want? Why do you follow us?"

Bill's mouth worked, but nothing came out. He didn't know what to say; all he knew at the moment was that he wanted his son back.

"Do you want to bring us harm?" the voice asked with a

sarcastic lilt. "Do you want to bring harm to your own kind?"

"I-I...I'm not your kind."

"But you are. You are."

There were more footsteps then, coming closer at a jog. And a voice.

"Jon? Jonny?"

Bill felt weak with horror. It was A.J.

"Jonathan, are you all ri—" She rounded the back end of one of the black trucks and froze, staring open mouthed at Bill, then at the thing that held their son between them.

A sheriff's deputy stepped up beside her, his hand fumbling for his gun once he realized what he was seeing.

"Okay," the deputy said, raising the gun, "just hold it there, just hold it a second. Let the boy go."

They can't see it, either, Bill thought.

The thing shifted in the darkness—it was an unnatural darkness, even darker than the shadows, that seemed to enfold the creature like a blanket—and Bill could see the glistening eyes turn to the deputy, who was stepping forward cautiously.

"You hear me?" he called. "Just let the boy go and we'll work this out without anybody getting hurt, okay?" Moving closer, he added firmly: "Right now." Closer. "I'm not playing with you." Closer still...Bill was going to speak up, warn the deputy, but what could he say? He was too late, anyway.

Something—Bill suspected it was an arm—whipped out of the darkness so fast that it was little more than a blur and struck the deputy in the chest. Ribs cracked like dry twigs and the deputy left the ground as if caught in a powerful wind. The gun tumbled away from him as his arms and legs flew out in front of him and his body shot across the aisle to the next row of parked trucks. His back slammed into the back of a trailer and he slid to the ground, crumbling into a rag-doll heap in the snow.

A.J. screamed. For a moment, she looked as if she were about to dive forward and attack the thing.

The big man behind Bill gasped, "Holy shit, what the hell is—"

Bill reached back and clutched the man's arm. "Get that woman out of here. Now."

He was around the truck in seconds, standing behind A.J. and holding her shoulders, trying to lead her away. He pulled her backward to the other side of the truck where her cries faded.

"Give me my son," Bill said, "and I'll do whatever you want."

"Join us," the black voice hissed without hesitation.

"What?"

"Travel with us. Hunt with us. You are endangering too many—yourself as well—by traveling alone. You are inexperienced. Ignorant. We can teach you. I can teach you. After all," it whispered slowly, almost sensuously, "you are one of my own."

"I don't need to travel with anyone. I've done fine for a year."

"Then why have you followed us?"

"To...to stop you."

It laughed. "Stop us? From doing what we must do? What you must do, as well?"

"No," he said, his voice low as it came through clenched teeth. "No, I don't kill. I don't hurt anyone."

"Then you will die!" the voice said happily. "You will grow weaker and weaker until you cannot move. And you will whither away. Surely you're feeling it already, aren't you?"

"No."

"Mmm. You don't lie well. You feed on animals? Or perhaps you steal the blood. From hospitals, I suppose. Many have tried that. The weak ones always do at first, the sentimental ones. But they soon learn that it is not the same. They grow weak, then ill. They learn something. You will learn it, too. Unless you feed on living humans, unless you drink warm blood still pumping through human veins and arteries, you will die. It is a wonderful way of weeding out the weaklings. Survival of the fittest, and all that. So. If you are not hunting, I do not believe that you are in good health." It laughed again. "You're dying already."

Bill looked at Jon, who seemed to be staring at something far in the distance; he seemed unaware of everything around him.

"Why was this done to me?" Bill asked.

"A mistake. It happens. It cannot be undone. You accept your situation or you don't. Which shall it be, Mr. Ketter?"

"Let my son go."

Bill saw the shadow-like shape of a long slender arm stretch out toward him in the darkness.

"Come to me first."

The black claws were smooth and glistening. The long boney fingers, skin flour white, beckoned gracefully.

"Dad?" Jon whimpered, as if he'd just awoke from a bad dream. "Dad? What's...what're you—"

"It's all right, Jon. Everything's all right." He tried to smile at his wide-eyed son, thinking that whatever was to come would be far better than watching Jon die. He stepped forward cautiously, nodding slowly, saying to the creature, "Okay. Fine. I'll come to you. But you've got to let my son—"

The enormous man appeared at the other end of the trucks, arms raised above his head, both hands clutching a yard-long winch bar. It remained suspended there for an instant, just long enough for light to sparkle on the chrome. Then it started downward.

The creature moved in a blur.

Bill cried out, "Nooo!"

Jon released a terrified, confused scream that was cut off instantly as he was pulled into the darkness and out of sight.

The milky white arm swept up, long fingers wrapped around the black man's wrist and he screamed, dropping the winch. It clattered to the ground behind him and he was pushed backward; he hit the pavement rolling through the dirty slush, grunting painfully until he slammed into the rear tires of a truck across the aisle.

"Not nice, Mr. Ketter," the creature hissed. "I've changed my mind." The creature swept around the back of the trailer in a whispering haze of darkness and Bill heard the door slide up with a rumble.

Feeling numb with fear, he stumbled forward as he heard Jon's cries cut short when his thin body tumbled into the trailer.

Bill rounded the trailer and looked into the square of blackness in which he could see, very faintly, a pale, hideous face, inhuman, with a glistening, grinning snout full of white needles.

He froze.

"Your time is running out," the face rasped, a thin pink tongue flickering behind the fangs. "You are growing weaker. You are becoming ill. You'll die soon. For good. You are no longer a threat. You are...a pity."

The door slammed down with a metallic explosion and then—

—the night was silent except for the wind that blew curtains of snowflakes in white swirls.

Bill's teeth crunched as they ground together. His fists clenched until his nails dug into his palms. He heard a low growl rising from his chest and—

—he threw himself against the trailer's door, his fists pounding the metal, echoing like thunder on the other side as he screamed incoherently. He grabbed the latch and jerked on it, throwing his whole weight into the effort. In a moment, he collapsed to his knees, weakened and trembling, his head hanging between his shoulders, chin pressed to his thin chest.

Behind him, the black man groaned as he climbed to his feet.

And a soft, sniffling voice whispered, "Bill? Buh-Bill, is... that you?"

Only when he lifted his head did he realize there were tears in his eyes and his stomach was hitching spastically, more from nausea than sobs. He looked over his shoulder to see A.J. standing a few yards away.

"Bill?" she said again, just a breath this time.

He nodded jerkily.

For a long time, they just stared at one another as the snow fell...

CHAPTER 12

Although it was a busy night at the truck stop, no one responded to the screaming and shouting in the back lot. The wind had picked up considerably and the night was a white blur of snow; the engines of both cars and trucks blended into a constant idling thrum and people at the gas islands had to shout to one another to be heard above it all. Even those who did hear the agonized screams of Bill and Adelle Ketter had other things on their minds...

Delbert Terry had been kicking back in his sleeper, huddled beneath blankets, warmed by his heated bed pad and reading a Louis L'Amour novel as he made his way to the bottom of his second can of barbecue flavored Pringles. One of those late night talk shows was on his radio and when he tired of reading, he'd listen to the lamentations of faceless Americans who had called the show's toll free number. He was more than willing to forego a hot meal and coffee inside the crowded noisy truck stop; he preferred the quiet, warm solitude of his sleeper. Besides...

...he was horny.

The knock on the cab came just as a woman on the radio began to sob because her white upper middle class daughter was pregnant by and in love with a black man who had just gone to prison for selling drugs.

Delbert smiled and put down his book, flicked the radio off and called, "Yeah?"

No response.

He tossed the blankets aside and got up. "What?"

"Want some company?" A small, thin voice. Young.

Delbert liked them young.

He opened the sleeper door and looked down at the small

girl bundled in a heavy coat. She smiled up at him, her face pale, eyes heavy with a sexy, sleepy look. Delbert leaned out, offered his hand and chuckled, "C'mon up, honey."

She was light as a feather...

Lumpy Turner met his company for the evening when he returned to his truck after dinner. She was leaning against his fender smoking a cigarette, apparently unaware of the snow and biting wind, tall and slender with a face like a movie star—a little on the pasty side, but damned fine—and lips that set Lumpy's imagination racing.

"What can I do you for, missy?" Lumpy asked with a grin, knowing what he wanted to do her for.

When she spoke, the wind whipped smoke from her mouth violently: "You can start by opening up and letting me in."

"Fine by me, honey," Lumpy laughed, fishing his keys from his pocket...

While Lumpy Turner was taking his clothes off, a young-looking girl was wandering through the maze of trucks in the back lot. She moved casually, wearing jeans and a dark sweater that showed off her curves, hands clasped behind her back. She had red hair that framed her face in full, bouncing curls and waves. Her name was Victoria. She approached a truck that had a sticker on the door of the sleeper. The sticker showed a picture of a green lizard; around the lizard was drawn a red circle with a slash through it. Beside the circle was written NO LOT LIZARDS. She read it and chuckled before knocking on the door. There was movement inside and the door opened. A fat man, probably in his late fifties, wearing a sweatshirt and jeans, opened the door and smiled down at her.

"Want some company?" Victoria asked.

He shook his head slowly. "Didn't'cha read the sticker, honey?" he asked gently. "I don't do that sorta thing. I'm a Christian."

Victoria grimaced. "Fine."

The man nodded, waved and, still smiling, closed the door.

She moved to the next truck, knocked on the door and, when the man opened the door, he smiled and said, "You look cold, baby. You wanna come inside?"

She nodded and he reached down to help her up...

At that very moment, Joe Grimes was kneeling in his sleeper behind a girl on her hands and knees, both of them naked; Joe was clutching her long hair in his fist and sweating as his hips thrust forward again and again and again and he whimpered as the girl reached back between her legs and ran her fingernails over his swinging balls until she pulled away suddenly, rolled over and pulled him down on top of her growling, "In me, inside me now," as she wrapped her slender arms and legs around him and pressed her cool wet mouth to his throat...

And in a truck in another part of the lot, Warren Philpott lay on his back in his sleeper, trying to lift his head between the legs of the girl lying on top of him, but finding himself growing weak and dizzy and, oddly enough, nearing orgasm as the girl ground her mouth against his groin, making loud wet slurping sounds...

Each of them heard some or all of the incident that took place between the two Carsey Bros, trucks, but they heard it only vaguely. Their minds were on other things.

By the time the truck stop was plunged into utter blackness, Delbert Terry and Lumpy Turner and Joe Grimes and Warren Philpott, as well as many others on the lot, were unconscious and bleeding. All of their money and everything of value that could be removed from the cab were gone...

As the pale, young-looking girls prowled the back lot, knocking on cab after cab and offering companionship, Claude Carsey woke with blood in his eyes and reached up slowly with a trembling hand to wipe it away, but another hand—cool and small—took his wrist gently and pulled it away. A soft cloth dabbed at the blood, clearing it away until his eyes fluttered open and—

—in a fit of panic, Claude flailed his arms and legs, trying to back away from the girl as he made little huffing sounds of panic but his back was pressed against a stack of wooden crates and there was nowhere to go.

"You get your—don't you tuh-tuh—you keep away from me!" Claude sputtered in a high voice, slapping the girl's hand away.

She backed away, giggling. "Just trying to help," Amy said.

Claude's head throbbed and blood still dribbled from the wound on his forehead, but the pain was eclipsed by his revulsion at being touched by the girl...by one of them. Simply being so close to one of them made him shudder. He struggled to his feet, looking around, but the room spun and the floor tilted and he slid back down the crates onto his ass. He held his head between both hands and groaned, "Oh... oh, God... oh..."

Amy squatted down before him, clasped her hands between her knees, smiling. It was a big smile that showed her fangs. "Not feeling too well, Mr. Carsey?"

The smile didn't fool him. He knew she hated him. They all hated him. They hated Phil, too. But they needed both of them, so the truck drivers were tolerated. But only barely. Sometimes he saw the way they looked at him, the way they watched him when they thought he didn't notice, and those looks haunted his sleep...what little he got.

Claude wanted out. He'd wanted out so bad for so long that he couldn't remember why he'd gone along with the whole thing in the first place. It was sick and, worst of all, deadly. And for the money they got from the girls' little late night excursions in one truck stop after another, it certainly wasn't all that profitable considering the fear that came with it all. Fear of his own brother as well as those...things. The constant fear.

And now he was here with Amy, probably the worst of them all; there seemed to be something different about her, something...restless and angry.

"Go away," he said, his voice hoarse. "Get away from me, just go away."

"Sorry, but—" She shrugged, raising her brows helplessly. "—we're kinda stuck here, you and me."

"What? Where? Where are we?" He tried to get up again but the dizziness showed him back to his seat.

"In the basement of the restaurant. I think. Don't quote me."

"Well... I gotta go. I gotta get back to—" He was about to say he had to get back to his brother before Phil got pissed—Phil was pissy all the time, but when he really got pissed, death became a nice thought and Hell seemed like a vacation paradise—but something occurred to him. Maybe he shouldn't say anything. Maybe Amy was chummy with that guy who'd chased him and had, apparently, put him in this dark chilly place. After all, he—whoever he was—was one of them. Maybe something was going on...something bad. Maybe they were planning something. That was a thought that frosted Claude Carsey's heart.

He tried to relax, but couldn't and pressed his stiff back hard against the crates to get as far from her as possible.

She only leaned closer. Smiling again. That sharp-fanged smile that was like an ad for Satan's very own brand of toothpaste. "It's just you and me, Claude. All alone. At least for a while. I got a friend now, see? Someone you don't know. Your stinking brother, either. In fact, none of you know him, including that fucking freak you cart around in your truck." Still smiling around the bile in her voice: "Somebody who likes me. He's gonna do things for me, Claude. And he's coming soon." She leaned very close, only inches from his face, and there was a smell...It wasn't her breath, because they really didn't have any breath; it was just a faint smell that sort of wafted up from deep inside her—the smell of old meat covered with spoiled preserves—and it made Claude's face screw up. "Then...when he gets here... I figure we can have a little fun. The three of us."

Claude used to believe in God as a child. He'd gone to Sunday school and church with his parents and sung songs about Jesus. That had been a long time ago and the past few years had convinced him that there couldn't possibly be a God. But now Claude did something he hadn't done in over forty years.

Claude prayed, and...

...as Claude Carsey anticipated his death—or perhaps, God forbid, something worse—Jon Ketter sat with his knees hugged to his chest in the complete blackness of Claude's trailer. He could see nothing, but he knew he was not alone.

"You are afraid," the creature hissed. "You are trembling."

Jon said nothing. He stared in the direction of the voice, but saw only solid darkness.

"You should not be afraid." There was a smile in the voice. "I will not hurt you. Your father is the one I want. He should be with us. He needs to be with us. He will die alone. And he may expose us. But you... you are safe here. Don't be afraid." Jon felt a thin ice cold finger stroke his jawline gently and the tip of a claw run over his skin. The creature said, with a soft, feminine chuckle, "You are too old for me."

But he was afraid. He could not move, couldn't even think. He just stared into the darkness trembling, his body crawling with gooseflesh and...

...Shawna Lake crawled with gooseflesh, too, as she stood at the living room window staring into the night. Grace Tipton was on the sofa doing a crossword puzzle as cartoons blared on the television. Moments before, Shawna had been seated in front of the television, legs crossed Indian style, watching Bugs Bunny and Elmer Fudd. But her attention had been elsewhere; it had been on the knot in her gut, on the gnawing certainty that something wasn't right. She'd finally been drawn to the window, as if she might be able to look outside and see whatever was wrong, whatever was disturbing her.

Mrs. Tipton joined her soon, touching her frail shoulder softly. "What's so interesting out there, Shawna?" she asked.

Shawna shrugged, but said nothing.

Mrs. Tipton hunkered down beside her, concerned, putting an arm around her waist. "Are you sure you feel all right, honey?"

Shawna was frowning, her lower lip tucked between her teeth. "I'm not sick. It's just that...something's wrong."

"What's wrong?"

"I don't know!" Shawna snapped, more harshly than she'd intended, spinning to face Mrs. Tipton. Softly, she repeated, "I don't know. Really. But something... something bad is wrong."

Mrs. Tipton put her hands on Shawna's shoulders and said, "Listen, sweety, if you say something's wrong, then you must have some idea what. You're making me very nervous with this talk. You know, it could have something to do with your medication...the way you're feeling, I mean. It can do things like that, you know, just make you feel bad for no reason. Do you think that's it?"

Shawna shook her head and opened her mouth to respond, but was shocked into silence when the lights went out and the house was swallowed by darkness and...

...the back lot disappeared when the power failed and Bill looked around in the dark, able to make out a few shapes: the long rectangular hulks of the trucks, the tall darkened mercury lights that stood like sleeping guards overlooking the lot and, deep within the maze, visible only now and then, petite, thin figures wandering around between the trucks.

"Oh, my Lord, what is happening around here?" the black man shouted.

There were other voices in the darkened lot, truckers grumbling about the outage, faint and whipped away by the wind, but none as loud or as filled with fear.

Bill got to his feet, turned and spotted A.J. She was kneeling in the snow, both hands pressed to her face, watching Bill between her fingers; she was mumbling something into her palms, or perhaps just sobbing, as she shook her head back and forth, back and forth...

She pulled her hands away slowly and whimpered, "Buh-Bill? Is thuh-that you?"

He approached her uncertainly, trying to find his voice. "Yeah, A.J. It's me."

She stood and headed unsteadily toward him, saying softly, "What's happened?" Moving faster, raising her voice: "What have you done?"

Bill stopped.

A.J. rushed him then, swinging her fists before she even reached him. She slammed into his body and began pummeling his chest, screaming, "What was that thing, that fucking thing where is Jonny, you sonofabitch, where's my Jonny?" She screamed on and on, hammering him, and Bill tried to stop her without hurting her but she began kicking his shins and knees then and it hurt—it really hurt—and he was just too weak for it, both mentally and physically. So he slapped her.

A.J. fell on her ass, gasping her shock, and Bill dropped to one knee at her side, whispering, "God, I'm sorry, A.J., I'm sorry, but I just—"

She slugged him in the stomach so hard and so unexpectedly that Bill doubled over with a startled grunt. She was sitting up straighter to hit him again when a beefy black hand clutched each of them and held them apart.

"Don't you think enough people have been hurt out here, dammit!" he barked, shaking them. "Now knock it off before I hafta beat the shit outta both of you!" He seemed embarrassed then and dropped his hands, wincing. "I'm...look, I'm sorry, but I'm just, y'know, kinda..." To Bill: "Listen, man, that cop over there is dead. You hear me? He is dead. Now I don't know what the story is with you two and I probably don't wanna know, but there's one thing I do want and that's for you to explain to me what the fuck I just saw out here because I don't think I'm too fuckin' sure, you know what I'm sayin'?" He'd grabbed the collar of Bill's coat in both hands and was shaking him as he roared in his face.

Bill wrapped his bony fingers around the man's thick wrists and squeezed. He felt weak and looked frail—although his face was barely visible to them in the snowy darkness and for that he was thankful—but he had enough strength to freeze the black man and make him tremble with pain as he squeezed the wrist bones hard and harder.

"What's your name?" Bill asked.

Through clenched teeth: "By...ron."

"Calm down, Byron. Okay?" Byron stared silently for a moment. "Okay, Byron?"

He nodded slowly at first, then his head bounced up and down like a ball. "Y-yuuhh...o-o-o...yuh-yeah, okay."

Bill's mind raced. He knew he could erase the memory of the last few minutes from the minds of both Byron and A.J., but then he would have no one to help him. He needed someone to help him. He smiled a little and spoke softly. "Listen to me, Byron. I need you to help me. You, too, A.J." He turned to her; she was staring at him with a sort of horrified fascination. To Byron again: "I don't want to hurt anybody, Byron. Really. What just happened here—" He gestured to A.J. "—well… it's kind of, um, complicated. She's my ex-wife."

Byron nodded quickly, wide-eyed. "I kinda figured."

"Right now, there are a lot of people in danger, Byron. They're snowed in here, there's no power, and there are some people wandering around here who want to hurt them. Do you understand?"

"I think I do, yeah. Now, I mean, after that, yeah."

"Well, I think I might be able to keep them from being hurt. But you have to believe that I don't want to hurt them. And you'll have to listen to me when I explain this. I mean, you'll have to listen to, um…to some stuff you might not want to believe."

Byron nodded.

Bill turned to A.J. "And you have to believe that I'm going to get Jon out of there. And…and that I want you and the kids… and Doug…to get out of here safely."

She seemed shocked by his knowledge of Doug, but nodded slowly.

"Okay," Bill whispered, preparing himself. "Okay." As briefly as possible, he told them everything…

CHAPTER 13

Bill talked so quickly that he sometimes stumbled over his words and had to start over. He tried not to look at their faces, afraid that he might see disbelieving eyes and, even worse, mocking smirks. But when he looked at A.J., he saw horror and sadness and confusion. Seeing her again made talking difficult. There were so many things he wanted to tell her, to ask her, and he knew he'd never see her again after tonight.

After what that creature had told him, he seriously doubted he would be seeing anyone, anything, after tonight.

Byron listened intently, nodding and making small sounds of shock, but he never showed any signs of disbelief.

When he finished his story, he turned slowly to A.J. He knew he was still no more than a faint silhouette in the dark to her, but the horrified expression on her face suggested that she could see him clearly.

"Why… I don't understand why you didn't… call or write," she whispered, as if she hadn't heard his story at all. "You could've written, at least. And…if you'd told me what was wrong…I would've helped you."

"What could you have done?"

"I could've tried. I've…well, I…I know I'm the one who left, but… I've missed you. We all have. Jon especially. You're still all he talks about and he's always—" She stopped and her gaze turned to the black Carsey Bros, truck. Her eyes teared up again and her lips quivered.

"We're gonna get him out of there," Bill said, as firmly as he could. He reached out to touch her, but she shrunk away convulsively.

"I-I'm…sorry," she whispered, turning away from him.

"You say garlic might help?" Byron asked.

"I think so. At least, with the girls. I'm not sure about that thing in the truck. The queen. That's gonna be tough."

"Well, I know where we can get some garlic. There's a shitload of it in the basement of the kitchen."

"Can you get to it?"

"I'm the janitor. I can get to anything."

Turning to A.J. again, Bill said, "Look, you've got to tell Doug about this. Make sure the girls are with one of you at all times."

She nodded.

"And as soon as you can, get out of here."

"We don't have a car. We had a wreck."

"What? Why didn't you tell me? Was anyone hurt?"

"No, no. We're fine. Except for the car."

He looked at her a long time, then asked, "Is he good to you? This Doug?"

She chuckled coldly. "Sometimes I think he's too good to me. Like you were."

"Then I'm glad. I'm glad." He nodded and turned away from her, resisting the urge to touch her again.

"Look," Byron said, "I hate to wreck your reunion, but whatta you say we go down to the basement."

Bill started to reply, then remembered Claude Carsey. "Shit, that's where I put him."

"What?" Byron said.

"Carsey. One of the drivers. After I knocked him cold, I put him through a basement window behind the restaurant."

"But it's kept locked."

"It was open a crack."

"Shit. Don't sound good to me."

"Yeah," Bill said. "Let's get in there."

The restaurant was chaos. After the lights went out, a startled murmur passed over the tables and booths in a wave, then someone laughed, someone cursed, a baby shrieked and the auxiliary power clicked on. It sounded to Kevin like the curse came from Jenny. It came again.

"Shit!" she hissed, brushing by him behind the counter. She spun around and stalked back to his side. "Look at this." She waved her arm toward the crowd of diners.

There were only three auxiliary lights lined up over the pick-up window facing the dining area and they cast a harsh, shadowed glow over the tables. Each light was powered by its own battery pack—the generator had been stolen over a year ago and never replaced—and lasted only an hour if the batteries had been properly charged. A man shouted, "Shut those damned things off!"

"Do you believe that?" Jenny whispered. "He wants total darkness. Like this isn't bad enough." She swept a hand over her face, then back through her hair. "Do you know who's working the floor right now? Maybe I can get a cigarette break."

Kevin glanced at the clock. "I don't know, but I'm taking mine."

"What? You're getting a break in all this?"

"Hey, I asked for an early break about half an hour ago and he said yes. I'm gonna hold him to it."

She looked at him curiously, cocking her head slightly, as if there were something odd about Kevin. "You all right? You seem different."

Still thinking of Amy, Kevin smiled and nodded and said, "I'm fine," then headed down the corridor, punching out and grabbing the basement keys on his way. As he opened the door, he heard voices and froze. Had someone gone down there and found Amy? He'd be up shit creek if it was Craig. He quickly stepped through the door, closed it and peered down the stairs into the dark.

Amy was kneeling on the floor between the legs of a man slumped against a stack of crates beneath the window.

"Amy?" Kevin whispered.

She looked over her shoulder so quickly that her hair parachuted around her head. In the dark it was hard to tell, but it looked to Kevin like she was smiling. Grinning, actually. And there seemed to be something—two small things—hanging from her upper lip. Two small sharp things glistening with dark fluids.

She laughed.

"God, Amy, what...what're you..."

She stood and rushed toward him so quickly that he flinched. "Kevin!" she hissed. "You're back!" She wrapped her arms around him and held her face close to his. There was a wet, coppery smell to her breath that made him grimace. She seemed happy, giddy as a child. "I have so much to tell you!"

Kevin stiffened, backed away, but she grabbed his arms and pulled him toward her, whispering, "What's the matter? I thought you wanted to come down here so we could get close." She pressed her breasts against him and ran her hands over his chest lightly.

Kevin looked down at the man sprawled on the floor and a cold clutching feeling in his chest told him that something was very wrong here, so wrong that he wasn't going to be able to ignore it or walk away from it or keep anyone else from finding out.

The man stirred, his head lolled to one side and a booted foot scraped over the concrete floor.

"What's happened?" Kevin rasped. "Whuh-what've you done? Who's that man?"

"Someone who wanted to hurt me. Someone who's been hurting me for a long time. You wouldn't want someone to hurt me, would you, Kevin?"

Her satiny voice seemed distant and Kevin wanted nothing more than to get away from her, but he couldn't take his eyes off the man on the floor and that sharp odor he was smelling was beginning to make him feel a little queasy… and Amy was moving her hand down to his belt…then below his belt to his fly, where her fingers moved with purpose, pulling the zipper down with a hiss.

"Look at me, Kevin."

He did.

"You don't want to stay around here forever, do you?" she whispered, easing her hand into his pants. "You want to go away and see other places, right?" She began to stroke him gently. "You want to make lots of money, don't you? And you'd like to be with me…wouldn't you?"

In a heartbeat, the man on the floor was forgotten…

Mrs. Tipton touched a match to the last of three kerosene lanterns, casting a hazy orange glow over the dark room. "It's just the snow," she said, trying to sound cheerful. "Come over here by the fire and keep warm, honey."

Shawna moved to the fireplace, but kept looking over her shoulder at the front window. Mrs. Tipton had closed the drapes again and only a half inch or so of night-black space remained between them.

"What do you say we turn on the radio and see if we can find out what happened to the power, okay?" Mrs. Tipton turned on the small AM/FM radio on the lamp table beside her rocking chair. Turning the dial slowly, she stopped at each station and listened for a moment with a frown before passing onto the next in search of some news. A sound from the kitchen startled her and Mrs. Tipton jerked her head toward the hallway, then looked at Shawna and smiled through the murky flickering dimness.

"It's just the cat, honey," she said with quiet reassurance.

There was another sound, louder this time, a clatter, and Mrs. Tipton's hand jerked away from the radio. She turned to Shawna, her smile gone, mouth curled into a wrinkled little O.

Something welled up in Shawna's chest, a terrible thickness that made it difficult to breathe and she clutched her hands together. "Let's go, Mrs. Tipton!" she hissed. "Let's get out of the house! Now!"

The woman's mouth trembled into a hesitant smile. "Oh, sweetheart, don't be ridiculous. It's just Tug." She started to get up. "He's probably up on the counter making a mess and looking for foo—"

An even louder clatter was followed by footsteps.

Mrs. Tipton froze in a hunched, half-standing position, all confidence gone from her face. Shadows deepened her wrinkles and the lantern flames glistened in her eyes.

"Puh-please, Mrs. Tipton, we have to go!" Shawna whispered. "It's something bad, just like I said something bad!" She backed toward the window, chest heaving as she stared at the black hallway that led to the kitchen. The darkness oozed and Shawna threw herself at Mrs. Tipton, clutching her hand

and screaming, "Now Mrs. Tipton now we have to—"

They were in the living room in an instant, as if they had melted out of the darkness, two young women—girls, really—with skin like ivory, sunken cheeks and thin necks with muscle cords pulled taut. And they were smiling.

Mrs. Tipton screamed and clutched Shawna close to her side.

The girls moved toward them smoothly, confidently. One had blond hair and wore a long, tattered wool coat; the other wore a blue ski cap and a grey down jacket. The blond whispered, "Hi, little girl. What's your name?"

"You leave her alone!" Mrs. Tipton shrieked, stepping in front of Shawna.

The blond stopped, nodded and said, "Okay. What's your name, old lady?"

They moved quickly and were on Mrs. Tipton in a heartbeat, pushing her to the floor, embracing her, their faces pressing to each side of her neck as she struggled helplessly. Her screams were brief, and then she became silent, her wide eyes staring at the ceiling, mouth opening and closing like a fish out of water, hands clenching and unclenching, feet twitching.

Shawna held in her scream, hugging herself as she backed away clumsily until her shoulders were against the windowpane, then she spun around and screamed with all her might, pounding her fear-weakened fists on the glass: "Heelllp! Somebody heelllp!" She screamed the words over and over again until—

—hands clutched her shoulders and turned her around and Shawna looked into the white, smiling, blood-smeared face of the blond. From beneath her upper lip curled two long narrow fangs—just like the fangs on Mr. Edell's German shepherd next door—and each of them glistened with dark blood.

"Don't be afraid," the girl hissed, blood spattering from her lips. She pressed a bloody hand over Shawna's mouth, spun her around and embraced her from behind.

The other girl rose slowly, her tongue running over her lips, and stepped in front of them. Her eyes were heavy, as if she'd just awakened from a deep sleep. Her nose twitched a few times and she winced at Shawna. "She smells funny," she said.

"So?"

"I mean she smells...sick, maybe."

"Don't they all these days? She doesn't smell as bad as some. Probably just a bad diet. This is Hicksville, y'know. They probably live on grease around here. You bleed the old lady?"

"Course not, idiot. She's alive."

"Well, kill her. She'll talk."

The girl in the ski cap went back to Mrs. Tipton's side and the blond turned to watch. Shawna wanted to close her eyes, wanted to struggle, kick and fight, but she was simply too weak and terrified to do any of those things, so she watched as horror churned her insides. The girl bent down and held the old woman's head between both hands. With a sudden jerk, Mrs. Tipton's neck cracked sharply.

Shawna struggled then, tried to scream again, but only for a moment; she grew tired quickly and the girl's arms were like iron bars.

As the girls wrapped her up in two blankets, the blond smiled down at Shawna and said gently, "You're gonna come with us. There's somebody who wants to see you. Somebody who'll like you a whooole lot..."

CHAPTER 14

"Wait a sec," Byron said to Bill and A.J. before they went inside the truck stop. He jogged to a battered white Chevrolet pick-up, opened the door and reached behind the seat, retrieving a handgun which he stuffed beneath his belt under his jacket before he slammed the pick-up door and led them inside.

Inside, it was noisy and dark. They shouldered their way through the crowd, through the travel store and, after Byron stopped to get a flashlight from a utility closet, into the restaurant. Byron led them behind the counter toward the hall that led to the basement. A weary looking waitress holding two plates of half-eaten food stepped in front of Bill and A.J. and said, rather curtly, "I'm sorry, but you are not supposed to be back here."

Byron turned and put a hand on her shoulder. "It's okay, Jenny. They're with me."

She turned to him. "Byron, you look like shit. You okay?"

"Nope. Look, we' re going down to the basement. Anybody says anything, tell them they're with me and it's okay."

Looking confused and concerned, and glancing at Bill with a sort of sickened fascination, she nodded and hurried away.

"Bill?" Adelle whispered hesitantly. "I should go talk to Doug. He should know about...about what's happening."

"Okay." He squeezed her arm. "Remember, stick together and don't go outside, but get away from that guy at the next booth."

She nodded, looked sick for a moment, as if she might vomit or pass out, then began to cry quietly.

"Don't worry, A.J. We're gonna...we're gonna..." When she

looked up at him, he couldn't finish, he couldn't look her in the eyes and say it, so he held her to him, looking instead at a stack of dirty plates as he said, "We're gonna get him out of there and he's gonna be fine."

"Somebody mind telling me what the hell's going on here?"

The man's voice trembled only slightly with quiet, contained anger and when Bill turned to him, he knew somehow that it was Doug.

Adelle wiped her eyes and sniffled. "Doug, this is Bill. My ex-husband."

He said nothing, just stared Bill in the eyes. He looked angry at first, defensive, jaw set and eyes narrowed. But as he continued to look at Bill in the poor light, his expression changed to one of curiosity, then he backed away a little, frowning, all of his anger gone.

"We have to talk, Doug," Adelle said.

Doug's eyes darted back and forth between Bill and Adelle, suddenly worried. Her lips were quivering and she was about to start crying again. "What's going on here?" Doug asked.

"Just...Doug, please, come to the table. We have to talk." She sounded impatient. With another glance at Bill, she took Doug's hand and led him away.

As they started down the hall, Byron shook his head and said, "I bet you've had better days."

"Not in about a year."

Byron turned his flashlight on a ring of keys he'd taken from his belt, found the right one and unlocked the basement door.

"This is where they keep all the kitchen supplies and the food," Byron said, shining the flashlight into the darkness below as he started down the stairs. "The garlic's probably in the free—" He stopped half way down with Bill right behind him.

Sounds.

Movement.

A gasp...a sigh...a giggle...a low, gurgling whimper...

Byron swept the light around the basement until the beam found them: a boy and girl on a coat spread out on the concrete floor. The boy was on his back, jeans pulled down around his knees, the girl squatting atop him, hands flat on his chest as she ground her hips on him until she froze and they both looked up.

"Oh, shit!" the boy groaned, scrambling to get up. "Shit, oh shit, man, shit!" The girl moved off of him and he began pulling up his pants before he was off the floor.

"Kevin?" Byron asked.

Bill watched the girl...

"Kevin, what the hell're you doing?" Byron snapped.

...and the girl watched Bill as she slipped into her pants casually.

He whispered to Byron as he pushed by on the way down the stairs, "She's one of them."

Smiling, the girl swept up her coat, saying, "C'mon, Kevin, hurry up."

"Oh, shit, son of a bitch, I'm, shit, man, I'm fucked," Kevin rambled.

The girl's eyes remained on Bill's as he hurried down the stairs and her comfortable smile never faltered. As if without a thought, she bounded up onto the stack of crates beneath the small window, which she tore from its hinges and tossed to the floor where the pane shattered musically; her right leg kicked up expertly, her foot clanged against the upturned garbage dumpster just outside, and the dumpster slammed into the opposite wall, clearing the passage.

Kevin had stopped to stare in awe, his belt still unfastened.

Bill and Byron were halfway across the room, the flashlight beam dancing through the darkness.

She held out her arm to him and said firmly, "Give me your hand."

"What?"

"Give me your hand!"

Kevin did as he was told and she swept him off the floor, lifted him in both arms and pushed him out the window smoothly, then started to crawl out after him.

Thunder cracked in the room and a brief flash turned the walls white.

The girl slammed against the wall when a glistening

black-red flower blossomed in the middle of her back. She bounced from the wall, leaving behind a splash of red, and fell off the crates to the floor where she was still.

But only for a moment.

As the two men closed in on her, she sprang to her feet like a gymnast and hunched slightly, arms out at her sides, ready to defend herself. She was still smiling.

"Holy mother fucking shit sweet Jee-zus hear my prayer!" Byron bellowed, his feet skidding over the concrete as he quickly backed away, staring at the large black hole between the girl's breasts. He shined the light directly on the wound and saw that it was moving. Raw meat, shedding very little blood, was quivering...undulating...gelling...

His right hand, clenching the gun, began to convulse as he lifted it to fire again, babbling his horror in a high-pitched string of profanity as Bill dashed toward the girl from the side.

She did three things in the same second: she moved three big steps forward in a single leap, swung her right fist into Bill's chest, knocking him into the crates, and kicked up her left leg, connecting with Byron's right hand and sending the gun into the darkness. Then she slapped her hand over his face, pressed her fingers into his fleshy cheeks and pulled him toward her, getting very close.

"I'm already dead, you stupid nigger," she rasped, then slugged him in the stomach, slamming him into the wall beneath the stairs.

By the time she left the basement to join Kevin outside, the wounds beneath her tattered blood-stained clothes were healed.

As Adelle led him away from Bill and back to the table, Doug watched her and his stomach tightened. It had been bad enough seeing her walking through the dark with, of all people, her ex-husband—Doug recognized him from the family snapshots he'd seen—but the look on her face as she hurried stiffly—nearly jogged, in fact—around the tables and chairs told him that something bad was going on.

"Adelle, what the hell is the matter?" he asked.

She squeezed his hand. "Not now."

"What do you mean, not now? What were you doing with him? And what the hell is he doing here?"

She stopped and faced him. She was white with panic but managing to hold herself together. It wasn't until that moment that he realized she was trembling all over. "I'll explain in a minute, Doug, I promise I will, but first we have to get the girls away from that booth."

"Away from the—why?"

"That man." She nodded toward the booth beside theirs. "We have to get them away from him." Before he could ask why, she clutched his shirt in both hands, made a sound that could have been laughter or sobs... or both, closed her eyes and mouth tightly and took a deep breath, speaking quietly and with an exaggerated sort of calm. "Doug, something horrible has happened. Something I couldn't believe if I hadn't seen it. You know I don't panic easily. You know the shit I deal with in ER and you know I handle it pretty well but the truth is that I am about five seconds away from becoming a screaming convulsing vegetable and before that happens I want to get the girls away from that man and into another part of the building. Please, just please humor me for now and I'll tell you everything in a minute." Without waiting for him, she hurried to the table, leaned down and began gathering their things as she whispered to the girls.

Doug followed them out of the restaurant, stopping to pay their bill and glance back at the man in the booth beside theirs; he seemed agitated and was constantly looking around, as if waiting impatiently for his partner. Hurrying to catch up with Adelle and the girls, Bill went into the travel store, trying to keep himself from becoming too upset until he'd heard Adelle's story.

The store was lit by several lanterns and the two cashiers carried flashlights. People milled about in the darkness, their feet shuffling on the floor, their voices blending into a steady drone punctuated by an occasional laugh or a curse from a disgruntled trucker. Adelle went all the way back to the darkened soft drink coolers.

"Mom, what's going on?" Dara whined. "I wasn't through eating. I'm hungry."

Through clenched teeth, Adelle snapped, "Just be quiet and don't—" She stopped suddenly, flinching as if slapped. Her face relaxed and she put an arm around Dara, whispering, "I-I-I'm sorry, honey, I didn't muh-mean to bark at you like that." She embraced the girl for a moment, breathing, "I'm sorry."

This behavior worried Doug more than anything he'd seen so far.

"What's the matter, Mom?" Dara asked quietly. "You're crying."

Adelle backed away, shaking her head in dismissal.

"Mom," Cece asked, "where's Jon?"

Then she lost it. She buried her face in her hands, dropping her purse, and cried softly.

Doug stepped forward and said, "Look, girls, tell you what, since you didn't finish your dinner, here's twenty bucks. Get anything in the store. How about some junk food, huh? Doritos? Anything you want this time, no rules. Look, there's cold sandwiches in this cooler and drinks over here."

"Can I have a Jolt Cola?" Cece asked expectantly.

"Even a Jolt. Go ahead—" He handed Dara a twenty. "—it's on me. Your mom and I've gotta talk."

"No!" Adelle blurted. "No, girls, you stay right here, duh-don't move. You can eat anything you want, just do it right here. Kuh-keep the wrappers and we'll pay for it later."

They spoke in whispers as the girls ate, Adelle doing most of the talking while Doug stared at her in utter disbelief...at first. Then, when she told him about Jon: "Son of a bitch, where is he, Adelle, why the hell didn't you say so in the—"

"Shh, keep your voice down, I don't want the girls to hear. Doug, I'm telling you, there's nothing we can do. That thing is...I saw that thing and there is nothing we can do. Except wait for Bill."

"Oh. Wait for Bill." The churning of jealousy stirred his guts and he paced a moment. "What the hell's Bill doing, changing his clothes in a phonebooth?"

"He's one of them."

"One of—you mean one of those—oh, God, Adelle, you don't really believe that shit, do you?"

"Goddammit, Douglas, I don't know what they are and I don't care what you call them, but they're out there and he knows how to handle them. I don't know, maybe they're just like us and they've got some kind of-of-of horrible duh-disease or something, but that thing, Doug, I saw that thing, and if everybody here knew about it there'd be a fucking stampede, except nobody has anyplace to go! Now will you please for God's sake just—" She stopped again, grinding her teeth. "I'm sorry, dammit, I'm sorry."

Doug stepped forward and held her as she whispered in his ear.

"I yelled at Jonny. At the table...in the car...I yelled at everybody, even after the wreck, I mean... we all could've been killed, but I...all I did was yell. And now he's...if that thuh-thing...oh, Doug, I just can't live with the thought of my last words to my son being angry ones..."

Bill tried to get back on his feet immediately but was surprised by his clumsiness, by the drained feeling that covered his body, as if the attack had doubled the weakness he'd felt before.

"Byron?" he croaked.

"Yeah. Yeah, I'm here."

Bill saw the flashlight glowing on the floor, heard Byron shuffling around until he found it, then watched him retrieve his gun.

"I don't know why I'm here," Byron said, coming toward him, "'cause if I had any brains I'd get the fuck gone. You okay?"

"I'm...not sure. Don't feel too well, tell you the truth."

Claude Carsey groaned in the dark as Byron helped Bill to his feet. They went to Claude's side and shined the light on him. His face was bloody and his eyes gummy and swollen; he looked up at them with his mouth yawning and hands quivering.

"She killed me?" he rasped. "Am I dead? Am-am-am I guh-gonna die?"

Byron squatted down and touched Claude's cheek with the barrel of his gun. "No, you're gonna help us, that's what you're gonna do."

Getting on his knees, Bill asked, as firmly as he could

manage, "What does garlic do to them, Claude?"

"Gar...lic? Well, I s'pose you could find out easy enough."

"Remember what I just said about you not dying?" Byron growled. "One more remark like that and I'm gonna have to make myself a liar."

"Makes 'em sick," Claude said. "Ruh-real sick."

"When they touch it?"

"No, no. Tha's just when they smell it. Don't know what the hell happens when they touch it." He turned his head and spit some blood onto the concrete.

Bill and Byron exchanged a glance.

"What happens if they can't get back in the trucks, Claude?" Bill asked.

His swollen eyes widened slightly. "If they can't...I don't know, but it must be bad, 'cause that's the only thing they're scared of. Scared shitless of it. And why the fuck don't you know what hap—" He glanced at the gun. "—well, I mean...I figure you oughta know what sunlight does."

"Ain't gonna be very sunny out today," Byron told Bill.

Claude said, "Weather don't seem to matter to 'em none. Least not that I can tell. But...what, um...oh, Lordy, no, you guys ain't thinkin' of...no, you ain't gonna do that, no, you can't do that. You know what my brother would do to me? He'd fuckin' kill me's what he'd do." He sat up, pleading now. "No, please, you can't do that, you can't—"

But they ignored him.

"The other guy," Bill whispered. "We've gotta get him down here and out of the way."

Byron stood as Bill gave him a description of Phil Carsey and told him where Phil was seated.

"You gonna be able to handle this guy?" Byron asked, handing Bill the flashlight.

"Sure." Bill gave Claude a weak but toothy grin and said, "You won't give me any trouble as long as I promise not to give you a kiss, will you, Claude?"

Claude began to cry...

Byron hurried up the stairs, putting the gun in his jacket pocket, but never taking his hand from it. In the restaurant, he spotted the other Carsey brother easily and approached his booth casually. Standing behind him, Byron leaned forward and, through the jacket, pressed the gun to the back of Phil's neck, whispering, "Now listen, motherfucker." Byron knew that nothing struck fear into the heart of the average white man quite as effectively as a large black man with a gun calling him motherfucker and it tickled him. "You're gonna get up real nice and slow, like you and me are old friends, and you're gonna come with me across the restaurant to the hallway back there without doing anything funny, or my little friend here's gonna take your face for a ride clean across this building, you understand?"

Phil swallowed dryly and nodded, then, clumsily but with caution, scooted out of the booth and walked a step ahead of Byron to the hallway as the barrel of the gun bumped his lower back with each step. At the end of the hall, Byron removed the gun from his pocket, opened the door and motioned Phil down the stairs, calling to Bill for some light.

In the basement, Phil spat at his brother, "What the fuck'd you do, asshole?"

Byron poked him hard with the gun. "Shut up." To Bill: "Flash that around. There's some rope down here somewhere."

"Holy shit," Phil chuckled coldly at Bill. "You."

"Yeah, me. Sit down with your brother."

Bill got a fat coil of rope from a hook on the wall, handed the gun to Bill, placed the flashlight on a crate and wasted no time in tying the Carsey brothers back to back. As he grunted and strained, pulling the rope tight, Bill said, "Maybe you can give us a little more information than your brother could, Phil."

"Go fuck yourself," he gurgled.

Byron moved quickly, enraged; he slapped the gun from Bill's hand, dropped to one knee, grabbed as much of Phil Carsey's hair as he could and pulled his head back hard until Phil was gagging, then shoved the barrel against his throat, spraying his fat face with spittle as he spoke in a rapid continuous stream: "Now you listen to me motherfucker. I'm a little edgy tonight and I'd be more than happy to blow your Goddamned brains out right now because you smell really bad and better yet I know you'll die and after some of the shit I've seen tonight that would be a pretty fuckin' reassuring sight, but maybe you'd like it better if my friend here took a little blood sample from one of your filthy fuckin' veins like them bitches you been haulin' in your trucks do while you're sittin' on your fat ugly ass eatin' chili, huh, would you like that, you wanna see what that's like, huh?"

Phil's face reddened and trembled with anger, but his eyes gave away his fear. "Whuh-what? Whatta you want?" he whispered.

Byron let go of him, stood and took a deep, steadying breath, then handed the gun back to Bill and continued securing the ropes.

Bill's voice was unsteady: "That thing out in your truck has my son. I wanna know what to do about it."

Phil smirked. "Have another one."

Bill leaned close, touching his nose to Phil's and showing his fangs. "What...is...she?"

Phil's nostrils flared with disgust. "The queen. Sorta... sorta like their... leader, I guess. Their mother, kinda. She knows what they're thinkin', what they're doin'...least, she seems to. Hell, half the time, I think she knows what I'm thinkin' and doin'. I-I-I...look, I'm sorry, but...if she's got your son...you ain't gonna see him alive again. She likes 'em young."

With clenched teeth: "I want to kill her. How do I do it?"

"Yuh-you think I know? You duh-don't think I'd've tried by now if I knew? I hate that fuckin' thing, she scares the shit outta me, but there ain't a Goddamned thing I can do about it."

"Where'd you find her?"

"Oh, no. She found us. We...we was independents. Went all over the country haulin' shit. We was in upstate New York on our way to pick up a couple loads a pastries. Y'know, packaged shit like Ding Dongs and Ho Ho's. We stopped at a rest stop. Late at night. There was a few cars there, but...there was no people. Place was dead. Hah. Dead. Went into the bathroom and there they was. These three guys. Feet stickin' outta three different stalls. Blood on the floor. They looked dead. Claude got sick. I got scared. Ran outside and looked in them other cars parked in the lot. There was…more bodies. Never looked, but I figured there was more in the ladies' room. All I wanted was to get the fuck outta there, y'know? And then… there she was. Just as big and ugly as you please seepin' outta the dark. A great…big…Goddamned demon. Tha's what I thought she was at first, I swear, a fuckin' demon from Hell." He'd gotten out a breath and panted a moment. "Thuh-they'd been stayin' in this little cave way out in back of the rest stop. Made us go to a…a little cemetery way out in the middle of fuckin' nowhere. Made us…" He clenched his eyes against his memories, "…made us dig up coffins to haul 'em in. Wuh-we had to…empty all these fuckin' coffins. Practically dug up the whole place before we had enough. All those—oh, sweet Jesus—all those bones and-and-and cuh-corpses. Rotted and smelling and… the smell, man, you just don't know the smuh-smell." He stopped a moment, eyes closed, then: "Seven years ago. Believe me, buddy, if I knew how to stop her…" He just shook his head silently, eyes wide.

"Then why do you do it, asshole? Why don't you just stop?" He gave a soft, unpleasant giggle. "Hee… hee-hee…steady money and, uuhhh…hee-hee…lotsa travel a course, a-and, lessee…buh-because she, hee-hee, won't fuckin' let us. Never let us, you kuh-kiddin'? That…cunt…flies, man!" he hissed. "She's got fuckin' wings like a great big fuckin' bat!" His flabby cheeks quivered like gelatin, his eyes filled with tears and his shoulders quaked within their bonds.

Byron finished tying and stood slowly, staring at Bill with a look of growing horror.

Phil's words came in a wet, trembling breath. "I'm fucked, man. Me'n him both. We'll be doin' this the rest of our fuckin' liiives. And there ain't nothin' you can do… to stop it." He broke down then, sobbing openly, his chin pressed to his chest, head bobbing.

"Huh-hey, Phil," Claude whispered from behind him, craning his head around to look over his shoulder. "Hey, duh-don't cry, Phil. C'mon, Phil, don't…don't cry…"

Bill and Byron stared at one another for a long moment, both of them afraid to speak. Then Byron asked, "What do you suppose we should do?"

Bill massaged his chest with four fingertips; it felt empty, cold...decaying. "I've got an idea. First we'll have to get the keys from them, then take the garlic out there and put some in at least one of the trucks to keep the girls out...until sunrise if we're lucky. Just keep it away from me. I feel bad enough as it is."

"What about the queen? What about your son?"

Bill closed his eyes and shook his head slowly. "I just...don't know."

CHAPTER 15

Although she was wrapped tightly in a blanket with only her head exposed from her nose up, Shawna was not completely shielded from the bone chilling cold. But even the cold was overpowered by her fear.

She and the blond and the girl in the ski cap hid behind a large oak tree in Shawna's front yard as a group of three young people—two boys and a girl—strolled down the nearly deserted road in front of the house heading toward the truck stop.

"Oh, c'mon," the girl in the ski cap said in a voice that was no louder than the subtlest breeze, "they won't see us."

"They won't see us," the blond replied, "but the girl is different."

"Yeah, but you know how she gets when we're gone too long, and we've been gone too long already."

How who gets? Shawna wondered frantically. Who are they talking bout?

The ski cap girl continued: "I told you we should've taken one from the truck stop and—"

"And set off a panic? A search? While everybody's snowed in?"

The two couples in the road stopped for a snowball fight, then began making a snowman on the road's shoulder, laughing and exchanging jovial profanities, their voices carrying in the night.

So they waited for safety while Shawna trembled...

... and while Byron shined his flashlight cautiously into the trailer Bill had pointed out.

The Carsey brothers had refused to tell them which key opened the lock—Phil had said, "I won't tell you because I don't want to kill you. You wanna die, you figure it out yourself."—so Byron had tried one after another until one worked. Bill remained invisible in the darkness, keeping a safe distance from the garlic that Byron had loaded into two small heavy duty boxes. Bill looked bad, really bad, like he was dying—He's already dead, Byron thought humorlessly—and Byron was more afraid than he'd ever been; he was afraid that he couldn't do this alone if Bill died...in fact, he was sure of it.

Once he'd slid the door upward, the flashlight's beam cut through the trailer's blackness and spilled over shiny black rectangular boxes. Caskets. Maybe thirty or more. In nice neat rows.

"Hoooo-leeee shit," Byron breathed.

He and Bill had agreed, somewhat reluctantly, that as soon as Byron had put garlic in all the caskets they could get to, so the girls couldn't return to the safety of their truck before sunrise, they would have to explain the situation to everyone in the truck stop. Once the girls realized their predicament, they would try to come inside, so the rest of the garlic would have to be spread all around the outside of the building until after daylight. Then they would take it from there. They were afraid, however, that there would not be enough garlic in the basement to be effective. In fact, having looked over the supply, they were almost certain there wouldn't be enough, in which case they would have to enlist the help of the other people in the building. Both of them were afraid, however, that no one would believe them, that they would be up against a number of very annoyed, and perhaps very amused, people, not to mention a few pissed off truckers looking for a fight.

"What is it?" Bill responded in a whisper from somewhere in the dark.

"Well...if everybody could see this, maybe they'd listen to what we have to say. Caskets. Lotsa caskets." He hefted the two boxes of garlic into the trailer then climbed in himself, taking his .38 from his jacket pocket. Any one of the caskets could be occupied and Byron felt his knees trembling. He reached down with his left hand, which held the flashlight, touched the lid of the closest casket, waited a moment, then threw it open.

Empty.

Putting his gun back in his pocket, he scooped a handful of garlic cloves out of the box and scattered them in the casket, then another handful. Then he lowered the lid.

Bill had warned him that the creature in the next truck—the queen—might be aware of what he was doing, so Byron kept looking over his shoulder at the open door, nervous, afraid. But he continued what he was doing—putting two handfuls of garlic cloves in each casket—as quickly as he could, then scattered the remaining cloves around the trailer floor before grabbing the boxes and hurrying back out. He pulled the door down, hopped off the bumper and he and Bill returned to the truck stop to spread the news, wondering if the queen in the next truck had sensed what they'd done...

...and under other circumstances, she might have. But, at the moment, she was terribly preoccupied. With her hunger.

In the trailer with the creature, Jon was literally numb with fear; he could neither move nor feel his limbs and remained curled up in the dark, back pressed to the wall of the trailer. But he could still see and hear.

There was constant movement in the thick darkness and the sound of dry skin rubbing together, of hard claws clicking against one another. And the sounds the creature made in her throat...

Gurgling sounds...hisses... wet, bitter mumblings.

"'Yes, Mistress,' they said...'we'll be quick...you won't hunger long...'"

He felt the touch of her trembling fingers on his face now and then, like the caress of dead snakes, and she stroked his hair sometimes as she rambled on and on, her voice bubbling in her throat like boiling blood.

"I may not be able to wait child...do you know what that means? You are beautiful. Do you know that I can hear your heart beating?"

He said nothing, just held his breath for a long while.

"Do you know that I can feel your heart beating without even touching you? Do you know that? I could rip your heart out so fast you would still see it beating. I could feed it to you before you lost consciousness. Your heart...your beautiful beating heart..." Her voice became a terrifying growl, almost a rumble: "Where are those little sluts?" And then—

—silence. Nothing.

What's she doing? Jon thought frantically. What's she doing that's so quiet and why isn't Dad here and where did everybody go and WHAT IS SHE DOING?

The silence continued...

... as Jenny got a cigarette break and headed straight for the telephone behind the register.

"It's out," the cashier said as Jenny picked up the receiver.

"What, all of them?"

"All the ones in here, anyway. They're electronic, remember? All that computerized shit," she spat. "Might wanna try the payphone out front."

Jenny rolled her eyes and fished through her pocket for change as she pushed through the crowd toward the front entrance, not bothering to grab her coat.

Her whole body tensed when she stepped out into the cold. She squinted against the stinging snowflakes and cursed when her stiff fingers fumbled with the quarter then punched the wrong number into the telephone. She got a ring on her second try.

It rang four times. Six. Eight.

"C'mon, Grace," she muttered, her breath billowing from between chattering teeth, "pick up the damned phone."

A dozen times. Fourteen.

Jenny's throat felt tight when she hung up and tried again. Still no answer.

What could be wrong? she wondered, glancing toward her house. It was so dark, though, there seemed to be no house there at all.

"Oh, Lord," she said aloud, depositing the quarter again. "Oh, Lord..."

…inside the truck stop, Bill and Byron approached Adelle, Doug and the girls in the travel store and Bill explained what Byron had done.

Doug took Bill's arm and led him away to a rack of black Harley-Davidson teddies. Byron followed.

"Listen," Doug whispered firmly, "I'm not sure exactly what's going on here, but if this is some kind of prank, a hoax to get your wife back, or something, I'll throw you into court so fast you'll wish it had never crossed your mind."

Bill started to speak, but Byron beat him to it: "Hey, friend, if this is a hoax, it's got Allen Funt beat all to hell. Besides, I would've kicked the shit outta this guy by now, he was trying to pull something over. But it's no hoax and we ain't got no time to deal with you right now."

"It's okay, Byron," Bill said calmly. "Look, Doug, all I want to do is save my son, okay?" In a whisper, he added, "If that's still possible. Afterwards, you'll never see me again. I swear."

Doug softened then, averting his eyes a moment. "It's just… the whole thing is so—"

"—yeah, crazy, I know," Bill interrupted. "But we've gotta live with it." He slapped Doug on the shoulder and turned to Byron, nodding toward the restaurant as he said, "Let's go…"

…while outside, the blond carried Shawna effortlessly over a snowy field toward the truck stop. With each jarring footstep, Shawna felt colder and more terrified—even when it seemed she could never be more terrified—of her destination.

We're gonna take you to see somebody…somebody who'll like you a whooole lot…

…a whooole lot…

The way the girl had said it—with a voice full of meanness and a snide smile framing her blood-darkened teeth—made Shawna shudder more than did the cold.

They crossed the field diagonally, heading for the rear of the truck stop. After going over two fences and pushing through the surrounding hedges, they entered the back lot, creeping between the rows of parked trucks until—

—the blond froze, stiffened and pressed her fingers hard

into Shawna's back and shoulder.

The girl in the ski cap dropped to her knees holding her head and began to cry softly.

The blond staggered, trembling, and fell to one knee making grunting sounds. And then—

—it was over.

The girl in the ski cap sobbed.

The blond gasped, "She's angry. We've taken too long."

"I told you, dammit, I told you."

"Just shut up. We'll have to hurry, that's all."

Shawna was lifted again and the girls quickened their pace...

...as Jon's heart quickened its pace. The creature was growing more enraged. He sensed her moving about in the darkness, caught glimpses of her as she paced, heard her claws clicking together and her fangs making snick-snick sounds as her jaws opened and closed. She made a sudden movement in the darkness and Jon felt her hands on his shoulders, could see the vague outline of her head directly in front of his face and heard an odd rustling sound...like sheets of leather being shaken...

She stroked his throat and her claws scraped lightly across his skin. Her tongue, wet and cold, licked his cheek, worked its way down to his throat where her lips closed...sucked...

"Don't be afraid," she whispered. "You'll feel no pain. Only a moment of extreme—"

There were three knocks on the trailer door and she pulled away from him. The door rumbled upward and faint light penetrated the darkness. Two young women climbed in hesitantly, one of them carrying a frail little girl in her arms.

"We're sorry," one said, pulling the door down.

"We hurried," the other added, "but with the snow—"

The creature rushed forward and grabbed the little girl up in her arms, growling, "I don't want to hear excuses!" She backed away from the two women silently and stood still for a long moment, then the women dropped to their knees, clutching their heads and crying out in pain.

One whimpered, "Nuh-nuh-no, nuh-noooo!"

The other screeched, "Stop! Pluh-heeeze stop!"

Silence. The women fell back against the closed door, groaning.

"Get the light and turn it on," the creature hissed, turning to Jon, holding the girl close. "I want him to see this. I want him to see what his father really is."

There was a metallic click and light shined in the blackness.

And Jon screamed...

...as Jenny slammed the receiver back onto its hook and turned to stare out at the white-speckled night. The wind was blowing harder and snowflakes pelted her face as she tried to light a cigarette, cupping her hand around the lighter.

She had to get home. Something was wrong.

Stop it, she thought. They're probably all in bed—it's nearly three-thirty, for crying out loud—or maybe the weather's screwed up all the lines. So stop panicking.

But the sickening sense of urgency wouldn't leave her stomach.

Even if they were in bed, she thought, heading back inside, Grace would wake up and answer. And if the lines were down, I wouldn't have gotten anything at all.

She would ask for enough time to hurry home and if Dina didn't give it to her, she'd go anyway.

In the restaurant, Jenny winced against the three streams of harsh light, looking for Dina. She spotted her by the counter talking to one of the busboys, the newest one. Dina did not look happy. Jenny took a deep breath and approached her.

"...and if it took you that long to do it," Dina was saying quietly and calmly, "I don't know how you can possibly do your job competently. And frankly that worries me, so I hope you'll keep my concerns in mind."

He nodded and hurried away, and then Dina turned to Jenny.

"Look," Jenny said, "I know this is the wrong time, but I need my break now. I think something is wrong at my house. My little girl wasn't well earlier and—"

"She's been sick for a while, hasn't she?"

"Yes, very sick."

"Well then, it isn't unusual that she's not well, is it?"

"But no one is answering the phone."

"The phones are down."

"Not the payphones. I got a ring but there was no answer."

Dina frowned. "What exactly is wrong with your daughter?" she asked, folding her arms.

Jenny tried not to flinch. Had Dina heard something? From whom? Jenny wondered. She'd told no one what was really wrong with Shawna. Grace was the only one who knew. Yreka was not a town with a terribly open mind and Jenny knew word would get around quickly. She was afraid she might even lose her job and she simply couldn't afford that. So she told no one that Shawna's cancer was a complication of the AIDS virus which Shawna had contracted from a blood transfusion as a baby. Instead, she used half truths to answer questions about her daughter, as she did with Dina.

"She has bone cancer."

"Mmm. Well…try calling again and if you still don't get an answer…take a few minutes to go over there and check. But!" She held up a finger, smirked and narrowed her eyes slightly. "Punch out first. Do it on your own time."

Jenny heaved a sigh of relief. "Thank you. If I go, I promise I'll—"

"All right everybody, we need your attention!"

Both Jenny and Dina flinched and spun toward the booming voice. Byron was standing in the middle of the room with a gaunt pale man.

Dina muttered, "What in the hell is he doing?"

The din of the crowd lowered slightly, but most people paid no attention.

The man beside Byron started to speak but Byron touched his arm and shook his head. Byron reached into his coat pocket and removed a gun, held it up and shot it at the ceiling.

After a wave of simultaneous gasps, the room fell silent and no one moved.

"Okay, listen up!" Byron shouted. "We've gotta problem and we need the help of everybody in this room. Everybody in this building! We're all stuck here, right? We aren't going anywhere, right? There's been a spill on the freeway and it's closed and we're all gonna be here for a while. For hours. Maybe till sunrise or later. Now with that in mind, I want you to know that this guy—" He gestured toward the man beside him. "—has made me aware of a problem we've got outside this building. We are all in a lot of danger. Unfortunately, you aren't gonna wanna believe me when I tell you why we're in danger and all I can say is I sure as hell wouldn't be doin' this shit if it weren't true. So listen up! If you don't…" He looked around for a moment, almost as if he were uncertain of what he were doing, "…you're on your own." He turned to the man beside him and nodded.

The man seemed to think carefully for a moment, then took a moment longer to shift his shoulders, as if he were gearing up for something as—

—Dina walked away from Jenny, stalking toward Byron with a stiff back, head tilted back and chin jutting. She stopped two feet away from him, took a deep breath, held out a hand and said quietly, "Give me the gun, Byron. Give it to me."

Byron looked at her in disbelief.

"You know this will mean your job, Byron, unless you stop now." She waggled her fingers and stiffened her outstretched arm.

Byron sucked his lips in and his eyes became wide. "You can have my job!" he shouted. "You can have my fuckin' job after this! I quit! Now you—" He swung his arm up and put the gun in her face; his hand trembled. "—shut the fuck up!"

Dina's hand dropped to her side heavily and she backed up several steps, jaw slack.

Facing the crowd, Byron said, "Now this man is gonna talk, and if there's a brain in your fuckin' head, you'll listen to him!" He turned to his companion and said quietly, "Go ahead…"

… while Jon shuddered in the silent darkness. He suddenly had to urinate and the urge, coupled with his fear, was so intense that he was afraid he might wet his pants.

Once his eyes had adjusted to the light, Jon saw that the little girl was in a bundle beside him, staring at him with wide, watery blue eyes, her hands doubled in fists just below her chin.

But the woman-thing crouched before him was what frightened him the most. Her hair was black with grey streaks, disheveled and bushy, with some strands reaching her shoulders and others stopping at a level with her jawline, and it shined as if it were wet. Her nose was flat, its bridge lumpy with ridges and her skin, which was lined with wrinkles so fine that they resembled bloodless paper cuts, was the color of water-diluted milk and stretched tight over cheekbones that looked almost as sharp as the fangs that hung like slightly yellowed icicles between the thin grey lips of a pronounced snout. She was naked; patches of fine grey hair grew from her round breasts, swirling around erect brown nipples, and a strip of it ran down the middle of her concave belly between the ridges of a pronounced ribcage, blending into the dark triangular thatch that grew thickly between her stringy muscular legs. Thick black nails—like those that curled from her bony fingers—rose from her hairy toes and hunched over their ends, tapering to knife-like points. But the worst of it all, the thing that made Jon's mind reel, rose from behind her shoulders and stretched high above her head, pressed together and folded to her back, with black leathery skin as wrinkled as raisins.

Wings. Ridged bat-like wings.

The creature embraced the girl, lifted her to her breasts and leaned forward, opening her fanged mouth wide, her eyes never leaving Jon's…

…while Bill spoke to the crowd in the restaurant.

"Our problem now," he said, having spoken for a few minutes already to a roomful of silent, staring faces, "is to keep them out of here. Now, I think I know how we can do that. They can't—" He stopped, almost said "we can't", but decided against it; he hadn't told them about himself and didn't think it would be a good idea. "—they can't tolerate garlic. We've gotten a lot of garlic from the basement, but we've used some of it already and we don't know if there will be enough left to do what we need to do."

"A-and…what's that?" a woman asked timidly.

"We need to surround this place with it, especially all the doors and windows. To keep them out."

A bellowing laugh rang out and Bill turned toward the trucker's coffee counter to see a hefty man with a bushy brown beard, head back, laughing toward the ceiling. "Vampires!" he shouted jovially. "We got vampires, huh? Well, you're in luck. I gotta truckload a garlic out in the lot. Maybe there's somebody here's gotta truckload a crosses, too!" he continued laughing.

A scrawny fellow a few seats down spoke up: "No, no, don't laugh. It sounds right to me. I've been hearing stories."

"What stories?" the bearded man barked.

"From friends. Other truckers. About lot lizards who… bit 'em. Just like this guy says. And they stole shit from the truck. I always figured there was something weird about it, but…"

"Ha." The bearded man shook his head. "It's a fuckin' fairy tale's, what it is. Those girls just bit 'em because they was enjoyin' gettin' their brains fucked out, is what that was. And you can't tell me—" The trucker stopped mid-sentence when Byron rushed him, grabbed his head and pulled his head back, touching the barrel of the gun to his throat.

"You shittin' us about hauling garlic?" he demanded through clenched teeth. "You gotta load of garlic outside?"

The man nodded as much as he could.

Byron turned to Bill and said, "This is our man…"

…as Jon's eyes began to tear up. He whispered, "Please don't hurt her. She's just a little girl. Please—"

"She's exactly what I want," the creature said, her mouth inches from the girl's throat. "And this is exactly what your father will have to do to keep from dying. Because he's one of us." Her head shot forward and her fangs punched into the pale little girl's flesh.

Jon swallowed several times to keep from throwing up and closed his eyes, but he had to watch; he couldn't believe what he was seeing.

Blood oozed from under the creature's mouth and dribbled over the girl's neck; the girl didn't move, just stared blankly upward, mouth open, chest hitching. The creature's entire body moved fluidly as her mouth sucked. Her hands wriggled over the girl's body, stroking her face and hair and arms and—

—the creature froze. Stiffened. She lifted her head slowly, mouth open and dripping the girl's blood. Her eyes rolled lazily and her hands closed into fists as she sat up suddenly, holding the girl tightly in her arms. Her eyes were wide, mouth gaping, and then—

—she screamed. Her wings lifted and spread with a great rush of wind. Her scream cut through the air like a dull razor, growing louder and louder as she rose jerkily, her body writhing, and she turned, arms rising above her head as her scream became even louder and more piercing and—

—the little girl began to scream, too, her voice mixing with the awful squall as the creature turned and—

—dove toward the back of the trailer, scream rising, and slammed through the closed doors, wings spreading even further once she was outside and airborne. Her scream faded into the night as her wings carried her away with great leathery flapping sounds.

The two young women in the trailer pressed their backs to the wall, one standing straight, the other hunkered in a squat. They stared at the open doors with fearful eyes, trembling, the blond wringing her hands as she stood, the girl in the ski cap not moving at all. They seemed not to notice Jon at all.

Jon stood slowly, staring at the two women one more time. They were still staring at the open doors. He turned and headed quickly out of the trailer, running into the darkness.

An instant later, the two girls exchanged a confused glance, the blonde hissed, "Shit!" and they both jumped out of the trailer after the boy...

CHAPTER 16

At the very moment Jon dashed from the open trailer, Kevin's battered white Dodge pick-up was creeping farther and farther away from the truck stop, its headlights only barely cutting through the heavy snowfall; the chains on the pick-up's tires rattled and crunched over the deep snow on the road that had not yet been reached by the overworked plows.

Amy was pressed against him, one hand stroking his thigh—up and down, up and down, her fingers moving closer to the bulge in his crotch each time—and the other toying with his earlobe as she whispered promises to him, telling him of the things they could do together, the places they could go and all the things he could have now that she was with him.

Kevin had panicked when they were caught fooling around in the basement. He was sure he'd lose his job and probably have a hard time finding another one; Yreka was a small town and word traveled fast. But Amy had calmed his fears quickly.

"You don't need a job anymore," she'd said. "You have me. We're gonna take care of each other."

Although he had no reason to, somehow Kevin believed her. Her voice comforted him and he found himself wanting to stare into her eyes; her very presence made him feel better.

They were going back to his house so he could pick up some things to take with him. Then, as soon as the freeways cleared up, they were going...wherever. As he enjoyed the touch of her hands, he thought of all the places they might go, the things they might do, when—

—Amy stiffened beside him, her fingers dug into his thigh and she made a strangled sound in her throat.

"What'samatter?" Kevin asked.

She closed her eyes and clutched her head between her hands, hissing.

"Amy? What's wrong?" He pulled the pick-up over to the side of the road, slowing to a stop.

"Nuh-no," she barked. "Kuh-keep going!"

"But what's—"

"Just keep guh-going! Some-something wrong...with her... something huh-happening..."

"Something's wrong with who?"

Amy slammed her head against the dashboard and screamed, "Just get me away from her noowww!" as...

...Bill said to the patrons in the restaurant, "Okay, nobody has to panic, because we're ahead of these things! We've got the upper hand!" But they were starting to panic. Truckers at the coffee counter were starting to talk loudly, exchanging stories they'd heard from other truckers from around the country who'd had strange experiences with the lot lizards; families and couples were starting to rise from their tables to leave, moving quickly.

"No, no!" Bill shouted. "You can't leave! We can't go outside!"

Bill turned to Byron for help, but he was at the counter talking quietly with the trucker who had the load of garlic.

Byron turned to Bill suddenly and said, "Okay, c'mon, we gotta go out and get that stuff."

Bill held up a hand and started to speak again, hoping to impress upon the crowd that it was important not to leave the building, to stay inside, but he heard something. Everyone else heard it, too, and became silent, listening.

It was a scream. A horrible, piercing scream that was growing closer and closer, until—

—the silence was broken when an enormously obese woman stood at her table, knocking her chair over, and pointed at the window, screaming. Every head turned toward the window and more screams rose from the crowd.

At first, Bill thought it was a large bird, but that thought was so silly he nearly laughed out loud, realizing he should know better, and he dropped to his knees screaming, "Everybody get down!"

There was a clatter of plates and chairs as the crowd sought cover and the scream became louder and louder until an explosion of glass made it unbearable. With his arms over his head, Bill looked up.

The creature's mouth was yawning open, its eyes were bulging and it held a bundle in her arms. The bundle was screaming, too. It was a child...a little girl.

Screams rang out from the crowd and glass continued to shatter as the creature slammed into the lights hanging from the ceiling; shards of broken bulbs fell like rain.

And the creature continued to scream, flying in circles, broad wings creating a wind that smelled of rotting meat as the little girl in its arms cried like an infant.

"My baby!" a voice rang out.

Bill looked in the direction of the cry and saw the waitress who had stopped him and Byron on their way to the basement, her arms outstretched toward the creature, eyes wide with panic.

"My babyyy! Dear God, that's my little giirrll!" Ignoring the danger, the waitress dashed forward as the creature's wings faltered and it dipped toward the floor, still screeching hideously. "Shaww-na! Shaww-na!" she cried hoarsely.

Byron dove from his hunched position on the floor and wrapped his arms around the waitress's legs, knocking her down and holding her, covering her with his body as she fought to get up again. "Shawna! My baby! Please don't hurt my baby!" the waitress cried, as...

... Jon ran through the snowy night, the running footsteps behind him gaining rapidly. He tried to run faster, but the experience in the trailer had drained him, exhausted him, and he'd already pushed himself too far. His lungs were burning and his abdomen ached with the biting stitches of overexertion. He'd already started stumbling when he was tackled from behind; the second he hit the icy pavement with two arms wrapped around his knees, two more slammed against his back and held him down. He was gasping for air, but the two girls didn't take a single breath.

"Okay," one of them said, "whatta we do with him?"

"Don't know. Just...just, um...oh, shit, I'm not feelin'—"

"Yeah, me neither. What's...what the hell's happening?"

"I don't...know. She's...there must be...something wrong with...her."

The two girls began to groan and hiss. The hands lifted from Jon's back and his legs were freed. So exhausted that he couldn't continue running, he looked over his shoulder at them.

They were both on their knees holding their heads between their hands, their lips curled back to reveal their fangs. Their bodies convulsed as they pulled at their hair. The ski cap fell from one girl's head while the blonde clawed her own face with her nails, as...

...the creature swooped suddenly and clumsily, oblivious to the pleas of the child's mother. It slammed into a table that had been vacated only seconds before, knocking the table over and scattering its plates and glasses and utensils over the floor. The massive leathery wings lost their rhythm and, although the creature made a desperate attempt to stay in the air, it dropped the child to the floor and collapsed on the truckers' coffee counter, sliding a few feet, knocking aside napkin dispensers and coffee mugs and containers of sugar and cream. The wings continued to make feeble attempts at flight as the creature lay on its stomach kicking its legs and flailing its arms. It craned its head back, opened its muzzle-like mouth, exposing its glistening fangs and black, quivering tongue, and its eyes bulged as it released a long gurgling scream.

Byron was on his knees in an instant, holding his .38 between both hands as he shouted to be heard above the screams of the panicking crowd, "Everybody down, dammit!" Then he emptied the gun into the creature as it writhed on the counter.

When the gunshots stopped, the crowd became still and every eye watched the motionless creature. Slowly, it turned its trembling head to Byron, bared its fangs and made a painful snarling sound, merely angered by the bullets.

Several women screamed, including Jenny Lake who scurried over the floor toward her daughter, sobbing as she huddled protectively over the still little girl.

Byron got to his feet and staggered backward as he fumbled with the box of bullets in his jacket pocket, gawking in horror at the creature as it struggled off the counter, fell over the stools to the floor and began to crawl toward him.

The screaming grew louder; grown men cried out like little boys and children huddled under tables, their feet crunching over broken glass on the floor.

"Son of a bitch!" Byron shouted, spilling bullets from the small box. "Oohh momma sonofabitch!"

Bill stood as Byron neared him and watched the thing on the floor. Something was happening. In the harsh glow of the auxiliary lights, the creature was changing.

Byron dropped the box of bullets and it split open, sending its contents rolling over the carpet. "Shit, oh shit!" he shouted, backing into Bill, who clutched his arm and hissed, "Look!"

The creature's entire body was quivering like gelatin as it pulled itself over the floor, gagging and spitting as it dragged its wilted wings behind it. Its claws tore into the carpet and its fangs clacked together as it snapped at Byron. Beneath a sheen of fine greyish hair, the creature's pale skin was darkening and shriveling like the skin of a raisin; it seemed to thicken as it curled and wrinkled into a callous-like coating over the boney body and the creature's face became skull-like, resembling the head of a long-dead dog, its bulging eyes sinking rapidly into deepening sockets, its cheeks becoming caverns that flanked a thinning muzzle of fangs that yellowed and began to fall out, first one at a time, then several at a time, until the thin, black lips were pulling back over pathetic, shriveled gums. Sores blossomed like flowers over the creature's body and dribbled viscous fluids to the floor. The sounds it made became thinner and scratchier as it reached a trembling stick-like arm toward Byron, who took a few more steps backward and then—

—the creature's tortured eyes moved from Byron to Bill. It froze for a moment, its arm outstretched, fingers splayed; then it closed a fist, moving its arm slowly and pointing a long, knife-like index finger at Bill. It remained that way for a long moment as its body continued to decay, its wings curling into long strips of burnt paper, the hair falling away to form a grey pool around its body; the creature's lips moved around its smile as if it were about to speak, then, weakening, it settled for a simple quiet laugh as its eyes melted from their sockets and dribbled down the creature's cheeks like milky tears and its smile disappeared as its jaw dropped to the floor, leaving behind half a face. In spite of the crowd's loud panic, Bill heard the soft, wet crunch of the creature's neck severing as its head dropped away from its shoulders, hit the floor and rolled for a few inches, stopping near Bill's feet, its empty sockets staring blindly at him. Its arms snapped at the joints and the shriveling, glistening body began to collapse like a deflating balloon, releasing vile odors that made a few people retch. Its blackened skin became flakes that left behind bones which quickly crumbled like chalk into countless small dry pieces which crumbled further until nothing was left but dust in a puddle of bodily fluids surrounded by grey hairs that blew in the icy wind that came in through the broken window.

The room fell silent except for a few sobs and the sounds of sickness. Then the crowd began to talk among themselves, their voices rising slowly, the panic of a few moments before replaced now with confusion and fear.

"What the hell happened?" Bill whispered.

"I don't give a damn," Byron gasped, trying to catch his breath. "I'm just glad it did, is all."

"Oh God, somebody help my baby!" Jenny Lake cried, kneeling beside her daughter. "She's bleeding! She's been hurt! Oh God, I think she's been—"

Jenny was interrupted mid-sentence by a sound from outside. It began faintly, then grew louder as it became more identifiable: a high-pitched shriek. All eyes turned from the heap of moist, blackened ashes to the broken window through which gusts of snow still blew. The shriek was joined by another, and another, until the night was singing with a chorus of bone-chilling, not-quite-human screams. And among them, so faint that it was almost buried, was a voice that made Bill's heart skip a beat; it was crying, "Daaaad! Daaaad!"

A.J. hurried into the restaurant, her voice weak as she

stammered, "Bill? Was thuh-that him? Wuh-was that our Juh-Jonny?"

Bill turned to Byron and snapped, "Bring some garlic," as he headed past A.J. and out of the restaurant.

Byron vaulted over the coffee counter to one of the remaining crates of garlic, put down his gun for a moment and began stuffing fistfuls of it into his pockets. He stuffed his gun under his belt, picked up the crate and said to the trucker who'd said he was hauling garlic, "Grab one of these and follow me." Then, to the crowd: "We're gonna need all the help we can get! Anybody interested in all of us staying alive, come out and give a hand." Then he followed Bill at a jog, as...

... Jon crawled frantically over the snow, trying to get away from the two girls who were now wailing like a couple of tortured animals, dragging their nails over their own skin and opening bloodless cuts in their faces. One of them, the blonde, looked at Jon with eyes stretched open so wide he was surprised her eyeballs didn't pop from their sockets and, like a stalking cat about to pounce, she crawled over the snow toward him, her mouth gaping, fangs glistening with saliva as she hissed and snarled, spittle dribbling from her lips, while the girl behind her clawed at her own eyes until her fingers were wet with viscous fluids and her sockets were gushing holes, and—

—Jon stumbled to his feet, screaming for his dad again, as screams of agony rose in the dark around him, female voices wailing as if their flesh were being burned off, and—

—there were male voices, too, crying out in fear and pain, and—

—women began to fall from the cabs of the trucks in the parking lot and ran, screaming, through the snow all around him, running as if pursued by their worst nightmares, their arms outstretched, some of them naked or only half dressed, with garments hanging from their bodies as if they had suddenly gone mad in the act of undressing, and—

—the blonde dove forward, clutching the cuffs of Jon's pants, nearly tripping him up before he could start running, and his cries for his dad collapsed into senseless screams of terror, when—

—two arms wrapped around him suddenly from behind, pulled him away from the girl and threw him aside.

Jon's screams became quiet sobs of relief when he saw that it was his dad. He kicked the girl in the face, surprising her enough to knock her backward with a shocked grunt. He grabbed Jon's elbow and began leading him toward the building as he said, "Are you all right?"

Unable to form words yet, Jon simply nodded as he and his dad hurried into the truck stop. His dad looked back over his shoulder at the figures staggering and running and crawling in the night.

The big black man Jon had seen with Dad earlier was hurrying out the door as they went in and his dad said to him, "Get that garlic around the windows. They're everywhere and they've gone crazy."

Several men followed the black man out of the building, all of them shouting confused questions and barking curses as they ran toward the lot.

Inside, Jon's mom rushed toward him, crying his name as she embraced him and held him tighter than he could remember ever being held.

"Oh Jonny," she cried, "oh thank God, Jonny, I'm sorry, I'm so sorry I yelled at you, thank God, are you all right, honey, are you hurt, did that thing hurt you?"

Jon felt confused suddenly, as if he'd just awakened from a deep sleep, and stared silently for a moment at all the people standing around in the dark staring at him. They all looked so scared.

"No," he muttered when Mom pulled back to look at him. "No, Mom, I'm not hurt. But there was... a little girl," he added, frowning, as...

...Kevin began to panic, swerving the pick-up over the icy road as Amy screamed endlessly, slamming herself around in the cab, pounding her fists on the door and window, digging her nails into the dashboard and seat, ripping out chunks of vinyl. Kevin shouted for her to stop or tell him what was wrong, or something, anything, but she seemed unaware of his presence.

Finally, he tried to concentrate solely on regaining control of the careening pick-up, but—

—it was too late, and the tires slid over ice at an angle across the road, dumping the Dodge into the ditch on the opposite side.

"Amy!" Kevin shouted, killing the engine and pressing himself against the door to get as far from her as possible until she calmed down. "Amy, what the hell is wrong? Stop it!" But she ignored him, or didn't hear him, and continued thrashing around in the cab, slapping and scratching herself, clutching her hair and pulling her fists away with knotted strands sticking between her fingers, and her screams sometimes formed garbled words and, stiff with fear and confusion, Kevin listened carefully, trying to make them out:

"—how—die—could sh—ow could—eee die—how cuh—could she—die—"

How could she die?

Kevin squinted, puzzled, as he reached for the door handle behind him, hoping to slip out and head back toward the truck stop on foot, because it was obvious to him now that he'd made a big mistake in taking off with this girl, because she was out of her fucking mind, she was loopier than a roller coaster, and his sweating fingers closed around the handle, pulled up on it and—

—that was when silence fell in the cab for just a moment and that was when she turned to him and froze, just staring, her skin whiter than before, her eyes deeper, her hair splayed around her head in a swarm of Medusa-like snakes, and—

—that was when she dove toward him, arms outstretched, and they both tumbled out the door and into the snow, where—

—Kevin felt her teeth sink into his shoulder, then into his neck, and her nails scraped his face and she clutched his hair, pulling his head back hard until his throat was completely exposed and Amy lifted her head, opened her mouth wide, snarling deep in her throat, as—

—he became oddly aware of the throbbing vein just beneath his jaw because that, he somehow knew, was what she was looking at as her face hovered above him for a long, slow moment, until—

—she dove forward and her fangs pierced his flesh and her jaw clenched and—

—Kevin's scream was drowned in his own blood.

CHAPTER 17

When Bill left Jon with A.J., he went back outside with the gut-level certainty that something was dreadfully wrong. Something had happened, things had changed and, although he wasn't sure why—although he knew he should be happy about the unexpected death of the creature that had taken Jon—he knew things were now worse. He walked along the windowed front of the building and rounded the corner to the back lot, and—

—he froze. The darkness was alive with movement.

Squinting against the stinging snowflakes that blew into his face, Bill saw figures zigzagging between the rows of trucks. Many of the figures were obviously men; Bill could tell from their size and the way they moved...and from their screams. They were screaming like terrified children. And behind them—all around them—were smaller figures: the girls. Some of them managed to make themselves invisible in the darkness to normal eyes—to the eyes of the living—but most seemed unconcerned with hiding; they were running maniacally through the night, flailing their arms and making guttural sounds as they attacked the men, knocking them to the ground and feeding on them voraciously...loudly...

Bill held back for a moment watching them, afraid of them, not sure what to do. What had happened to make them so bold, so monstrous? Could it have been the death of their queen? And what had killed her?

Trying to ignore his pressing questions, Bill ran unsteadily around the perimeter of the back lot toward the source of the sound. Suddenly overcome with weakness, he stumbled to a stop thinking, for a moment, that he was about to lose consciousness. Lifting a hand from his side, he saw that it was shaking violently. He fell backward and slammed against a lamppost, trying hard to stay on his feet as he groaned at the feeling of dizziness that struck him suddenly.

Just fatigue, he thought, just strain, that's all. Too much has happened. But he couldn't keep from thinking of what that creature had told him... that he was already dying... dying, this time, for good.

Moving slowly, Bill pushed away from the lamppost and continued walking around the lot. He spotted Byron with the group of men who had followed him out of the restaurant. The beams of their flashlights cut through the darkness like swords. Some of the men had climbed onto a flatbed trailer with wooden siding and were unfastening and pulling back the heavy tarp that covered the garlic while the others stood around the truck, taking garlic from a crate and scattering it over the ground around them to hold off the girls who were trying to close in. There were maybe half a dozen of them around the truck, but they were shrinking back, some of them gagging and falling to their knees at the smell. Bill spotted one of them hiding under the trailer; she reached out and clutched the ankles of one of the men and began pulling him under with her. The man panicked and began screaming as he fell to the ground and dropped his flashlight. Byron spun around, aimed the gun and fired twice into her face. Two small black holes opened up in her white skin and she shrieked, releasing the man's ankles and crawling back under the trailer. The man she'd pulled to the ground did not seem to notice she was gone, however, and crawled over the snowy pavement, still screaming as he rose to his feet and began to run toward the building. The others shouted for him to come back, but he had already gone beyond the protective barrier of scattered garlic and—

—they were on him in an instant like a school of piranha, ripping his clothes away to get to his warm flesh and the blood that flowed beneath it.

Bill hurried toward the truck, forgetting the danger that awaited him until he caught the smell, long before he was even close to the garlic strewn over the pavement. It crawled up his nostrils like flames, burned down his throat and into his lungs, made his stomach convulse and his skin crawl; his eyes watered and his tongue seemed to swell in his mouth. He dropped to his knees and retched, suddenly dizzy and close to losing consciousness.

"Bill!" Byron called. "Get the hell away from here! Go back inside and keep everybody in there! We'll take care of this!"

Bill lifted his head and looked toward the truck; the flashlight beams blurred through the stinging tears in his eyes.

"Go on!" Byron shouted, waving his arms.

Crawling away and finally managing to climb to his feet, Bill did as he was told...

When he entered the truck stop, A.J. and Jon were standing at the front of the store; Doug was behind them in the darkness talking quietly with the girls, while others stood around, stiff and anxious, keeping their eyes on the windows and doors.

"What's happening?" A.J. asked, rushing toward him. Before he could answer, she gasped quietly and said, "My God, Bill, you look horrible. Are you all right?"

He leaned against a rack of candy and chewing gum and chuckled. "I don't think so."

"What's happening outside, Dad?" Jon asked, stepping forward.

"They're getting the guh-garlic from...from the truck. So they can spread it around. The building. At the doors and windows, and..." He felt dizzy again and paused, leaning forward and holding his head in his hands. When he lifted his head again, he realized that the other people around him were closing in, their expressions fearful, as if they were depending on him to tell them something they were waiting to hear. "Luh-look," he said quietly, "everything'll be okay if we just stay inside. That's all, just stay inside."

"But what if they come in here?" barked a fat woman as she bounced a baby in her arms.

Other voices spoke up, asking questions urgently, but they all melted into a buzz in Bill's ears. He lifted his hands trying to appear comforting. "It'll just be few more minutes before they have that garlic spread around the building. Then there's no way they can come in here."

The voices quieted, making way for a scream coming from the restaurant.

"Help! Please, somebody help! She's bleeeeding! She's bleeeeding!"

Bill and A.J. exchanged a glance, then she turned to Doug and said, "I'm going to see if there's something I can do." Bill followed her into the restaurant, where the waitress was still huddling over her little girl. Bill put his arm around Jon as they neared the kneeling woman, who looked up at A.J., eyes desperate.

"I'm a nurse," A.J. said.

The woman swept a hand across her teary eyes and said, "She's been bitten. Bad. She's bleeding."

A.J. knelt down beside her and the waitress, whose uniform was stained with blood, grasped her arm. Her face screwed up and tears fell more freely.

"She has AIDS," she whispered.

A.J. removed the woman's hand gently and turned the pale, frightened girl's head to one side so she could inspect the wound. "It's not too bad," she said. "We just need to stop the bleeding. Are there any rubber gloves around here?"

The waitress thought a moment, then said, "The dishwasher," and hurried away, returning a moment later with a pair of green latex dish washing gloves. As A.J. put them on, she said, "Get me a cloth, something clean to stop the flow, some hydrogen peroxide from the store, maybe, and some gauze if they have any."

The little girl blinked as her mother rushed to get the peroxide and bandages; she looked at A.J., confused and frightened, and asked, "Is the monster gone?"

With tears in her eyes, A.J. looked up at Bill, silently asking him for help. He hunkered down beside the girl and tried to sound reassuring as he said, "Yeah, honey. The monster's gone."

The girl squinted at Bill for a moment, asked his name and, after he'd replied, she asked, "Are you sick, too?"

Bill's lips pursed and he tried hard to swallow the viscous lump in his throat—

—You're dying already—

—as he nodded. "Yeah," he whispered. "I'm sick, too." He stood and turned to the crowd in the restaurant. They were watching him quietly with expectant eyes. "Everything's going to be okay," Bill said, "as long as none of you leave the building for any reason whatsoever. Just…stay inside."

The batteries powering the auxiliary lights finally died and the restaurant flickered into darkness. "Somebody get some of those halogen lanterns and bring them in here," Bill called weakly to no one in particular.

"What's gonna happen, Dad?" Jon asked quietly.

"We're going to stay here until sunrise, Jonny. It's just—" He glanced at his watch. "—oh, an hour or so from now. Things are going to be fine."

"No. I mean, what's gonna happen to you?"

Bill put his hand on Jon's shoulder and gave a closed-mouth smile. "Oh, don't worry about me. Tell you what. Go see how your sisters are doing, okay?" He patted the boy and gave him a gentle push. Once Jon had disappeared, tossing reluctant looks over his shoulder, Bill went to the coffee counter and fell heavily onto one of the stools, folding his arms on the counter and resting his head. "Good question," he mumbled quietly to himself. "What's gonna happen to me…"

Sunrise was only a short time away.

And he knew that what the creature had told him was true: he was dying…

CHAPTER 18

Time crawled by as the snow continued to swirl outside. Bill stayed at the coffee counter with his head on his arms, his strength draining from him like blood from a wound. He lifted his head occasionally, partly to keep himself awake, but also to check on Adelle, who continued to comfort Jenny, the waitress, and watch over her daughter Shawna; when the girl slept, Adelle moved around the restaurant helping Dr. Phillip Kale—who was rather upset himself—to calm down those on the verge of panic and to tend to the cuts and scratches a few people had gotten from the broken glass. One woman, however, would not be calmed. Dina Bonnick paced around the restaurant, her face pale and drawn, eyes wide and darting, wringing her hands as she said over and over—sometimes in a quiet mumble, other times in an authoritative bark—"This is a mess...a mess... this place is a mess, where is the janitor, this has to be... well, somebody has to clean this up. I'm responsible. I-I-I'm in charge here and this place is a mess!"

The doctor took her aside, holding her arm and patting her back, speaking to her in low, soothing tones.

"But this could mean my job!" she hissed, jerking away. "It's a mess, just a mess!" She began to tremble then, from head to foot, and Dr. Kale helped her into a chair where she mumbled incoherently to herself, rubbing her thighs jerkily and wringing her shaking hands.

Everyone in the restaurant spoke in hushed voices. Someone had turned on a radio and conversation fell to a faint murmur whenever an announcer updated the situation on the freeway. A baby cried now and then; sometimes the crying did not come from a baby. The crying increased each time one of the figures rushed toward the broken front window snarling like a rabid animal, only to stop and scream or fall to the ground. A couple of times, one of the girls—No, no, Bill thought, one of those things—came dangerously close to diving into the restaurant and Bill was afraid panic would break out again, but each time, the creatures were overcome by the garlic that Byron and the other men had finally managed to scatter around the building. Occasionally, the wind would blow over the garlic and into the restaurant, making Bill's eyes burn and his skin feel as if it were shrinking dangerously all over his body.

When he came back inside, Byron had been visibly shaken. He'd taken the seat beside Bill and lit a cigarette, blowing the smoke out hard as he kept his eyes on the window.

"Gave these damned things up four years ago," he said, waving the cigarette, "and climbed the walls for a month. But on my worst day, I never wanted a smoke as bad as I did just now. It's a fuckin' nightmare out there," he whispered. "Them things have gone crazy! They're like a pack of wild dogs or, or... hell, like a school of sharks in bloody water. And if they don't get that damned freeway open so we can get some help in here..." Another angry burst of smoke as he shook his head, still staring out at the night and vague figures that moved around in the darkness. "Fuckin' bullets don't do no good. Nothing stops 'em. 'Cept that garlic. God, I hope it keeps working."

"Janitor!" Dina Bonnick called from across the restaurant, shooting out of her chair and stabbing a finger toward Byron. "Janitor! You, Byron!" Dr. Kale tried to quiet her, get her to sit down, but she just shook him off. "Where have you been? Clean up this mess right now!" She pointed at the scattered shards of glass and the now crusty puddle of black ooze on the floor. "That is your job, you know! You do want to keep your job, don't you?"

Byron stared her down, cracking his knuckles as he smoked. Finally, he whispered, "Whatta you say I go over there and toss that dizzy bitch into the parking lot?"

"Don't worry about it, Byron," Bill said. "Everybody's scared and upset."

Byron stared at the woman for a few minutes, until the

doctor calmed her down and got her back into her seat, then he put out his cigarette, lit another and gestured toward what remained of the winged creature on the floor. "The hell you s'pose happened to that thing?"

It was becoming an effort to speak without slurring his words, but Bill said, "I'm not sure, but I think it had something to do with the little girl it was carrying. She has AIDS." He looked at Byron. "It drank some AIDS infected blood. Maybe that was it."

Byron stared at the lumpy substance, frowning. He cracked his knuckles a few more times then, without saying another word, stood and went to the window where he stared out at the night.

Bill groaned quietly and ran a hand through his hair. When he lowered it to the counter, he saw thick strands of hair clinging between his fingers. Turning his hand over, he saw that the skin around his fingernails was turning an odd bluish grey and beginning to crack and peel. Funny, he thought, they weren't that way a little while ago... were they?

A hand touched his shoulder and he jerked around, startled, to see Doug standing beside him. The man's mouth worked silently at first, struggling to find the right thing to say, then he looked away a moment.

"Look," he said finally, "I just want to say, erm, that I'm sorry about, erm, not taking you seriously before. I thought maybe you were...oh, I don't know what I thought."

"Forget it. Really." Bill tried to smile. "It's not the kind of thing that's easy to take seriously."

Hesitantly, Doug took a seat beside him.

"How're the girls?" Bill asked.

"Fine. They're over there with Jon." He nodded toward a table where the girls sat with their brother sipping cans of Pepsi. "They talk about you a lot, you know. All three of them. Especially Jon. They've missed you."

Bill felt as if he were expected to say something, but only nodded, and his silence seemed to embarrass Doug. "What are you going to do for transportation once the freeway's open?" Bill asked.

Shrugging, Doug said, "Once the freeway's open, we'll be able to get a tow truck out here, I suppose. But if that takes too long, I'll probably rent a car and send Adelle on ahead to her mother's."

The two of them stared out the window for a while. Patches of the darkness outside moved, seemed to ooze this way and that around the parked cars like black mud, and Bill knew it was them. They were out there, waiting, thinking, deciding what to do, how to get inside the restaurant where a magnificent buffet awaited them, with desserts of children and infants...

An elderly woman in the far rear corner of the restaurant began to sing "Rock of Ages" in a frail, cracked voice and, a few lines into the hymn, others joined her, until nearly everyone on that side of the restaurant was singing, some with spirit, others in mournful voices that wandered off key.

Bill turned his eyes to Doug, who was still watching the parking lot. Not a bad looking man. He seemed nice enough. And he appeared to be protective over A.J. and the kids.

"How did you meet?" Bill asked. "You and A.J."

Doug hesitated, uncomfortable. "Um, at work. The hospital. I'm a-yum, an X-ray tech." His eyebrows shot up and he looked surprised at his own words, as if he realized he'd just made some horrible gaffe, and added quickly, "But not until, you know, until after you'd left, I mean, there was nothing between us when you two were—"

Bill closed his eyes and held up a hand. "That's okay. Don't worry about it."

Doug sighed as if he felt he'd failed to say what he wanted to say.

Quietly: "Do you love her, Doug?"

He became fidgety. "Yeah. I love her. Very much. And those kids," he added, looking Bill in the eyes. "They're great kids. But...well, you know, that doesn't mean you couldn't come around and, you know, see them. Like I said, they've missed you."

Bill ground his teeth and scrubbed his cold face hard with a trembling hand. He didn't want to hear what he thought was coming.

"In fact," Doug went on, "once this is all over, you could come by once in a while. Spend some time with them. I know it'll be uncomfortable at first, but I think they'd really—"

Bill averted his eyes, shaking his head vigorously. "No, Doug," he said hoarsely. "I'm sorry but no, that's…not gonna happen." He stood and walked away from the counter as…

…Jenny stroked Shawna's forehead. She was so pale, her eyes nestled so deep in her dark sockets. Blood had been splattered on her face and in what remained of her hair. Jenny held a cloth to the wound on Shawna's neck, checking now and then to see that the bleeding was continuing to slow. The skin around the bite had turned a mottled purple and yellow and become puffy.

"They hurt Mrs. Tipton," Shawna whispered tremulously. "I think…maybe they killed her."

"Don't worry about that now, honey. Just try to hold still and relax and—"

—stay alive, try to stay alive like you've been doing for the last year, Shawna, please—

"—think about something nice." The restaurant had grown so cold that her breath wafted from her mouth like a small ghost each time she spoke.

"It bit me."

"I know, honey, but that thing is gone now. It's not gonna hurt you anymore." It was such an effort to keep her voice steady, to keep from falling apart in the face of the possibility that Shawna's wound might become infected, which, thanks to the virus, could kill her just as easily as the cancer. She wished the nurse or doctor would come back; it was easier to maintain herself when they were there to help.

The man named Bill returned to Jenny's side and gave Shawna a little smile. "How's it going?"

"Okay," Shawna answered flatly.

Speaking in a soothing voice, Bill asked her if she'd seen anyone else in the trailer where the monster had bitten her. She described a boy and Bill nodded, said that was his son, that he was all right now, and asked if there was anyone else.

"Just two ladies. They were mean. They hurt Mrs. Tipton

and took me from the house. They were real white. Sick-looking, maybe. Like us."

"Okay." He patted Shawna's shoulder and said, "Don't worry about them. They're not coming in, because we've—"

Byron came to Bill's side and clutched his arm urgently. "Gotta talk a sec. I got an idea. C'mon over here." He led Bill to the coffee counter where they spoke quietly.

Jenny watched them, feeling afraid again. Was something else wrong? Had things gotten worse? She reached down absently and took Shawna's hand, squeezing it as she watched the two men, watched their lips moving so quickly, their brows frowning, heads nodding rapidly. Byron pulled something from his coat pocket, a small box; he opened it, reached inside and produced what looked like a bullet. Holding it between thumb and forefinger, he gestured with it, still talking fast, then paused, waiting for Bill's response. Suddenly, they turned and looked at her at once and moved toward her as Byron returned the bullet to its box and the box to his pocket. She waited, but they said nothing for a long moment, exchanged hesitant glances, then squatted beside her.

"Jenny, honey," Byron said, his deep voice soft and uncertain, "we're gonna need your help."

There was something about the way he said it that made Jenny slide an arm under Shawna's shoulders and hold her closer to her side. "What? I mean, how?"

Another pause, another reluctant glance between the two men. Then Bill said, "We think the reason that thing died—" With a nod toward the mess on the floor. "—had something to do with your daughter. It bit your daughter, and…she has AIDS."

Jenny's insides began to shrink with dread. "Yuh-you wanna use my buh-baby for some kind of—"

"No, no," Byron whispered, squeezing her arm. "It's just a guess, but it's all we got to go on, and in case we're right, and in case all that garlic out there don't work…well, what we need is… we need some of your daughter's blood."

Jenny's eyes widened and she held Shawna even closer, hissing, "Are you out of your fucking mind, you want me to give you—you think I'll—my God, how can you—" She stopped, took a breath and started to get up, telling Shawna, "You wait just a second, sweetheart, I'll be right buh—"

The little girl gripped Jenny's hand hard, harder than Jenny thought she could, and said, "They think maybe I killed the monster, Momma? That maybe I can stop the others?"

"You never mind, honey, I'm gonna go talk to these men and—"

"Is that what they think?" Her eyes were brighter than Jenny had seen them in a long time and she sucked her lower lip between her teeth, lifting her head from Jenny's rolled up coat, frowning.

Jenny glanced at Byron, then Bill. They both nodded. Shawna saw their silent replies and squeezed Jenny's hand again, saying as firmly as she could, "Then I want to help."

Bill and Byron sat at the coffee counter with the box of bullets open and the bullets lined up before them. Each wore rubber dishwashing gloves and held a cloth that had been soaked with Shawna Lake's AIDS infected blood. One at a time, they picked up a bullet, held it delicately between thumb and forefinger and squeezed the cloth around it, coating it with the blood; the bloody bullet was then returned to the counter in another line. As they worked, they watched the window, catching glimpses of figures moving in the darkness outside, watching them.

"This might not work," Bill muttered.

"How come?"

"Well, I don't know how long the virus will last on a bullet out in the open, know what I mean? And it's being shot through a gun. And a bullet isn't exactly a sponge. A bunch of reasons, know what I mean?"

"Yeah, yeah, we're grabbin' at straws, I know, but what the hell else we gonna grab at? Tell you what," Byron said, turning to him. "You come up with a fool-proof idea and I'll drop this one like a bad habit."

Bill nodded in agreement and they continued in silence.

As the minutes passed, Bill noticed his hands were trembling more and more. A knot grew in his stomach slowly but surely, becoming almost unbearable. It was a feeling he'd had before, a year ago, when he was unfamiliar with his condition. He'd always likened it to watching the most suspenseful scenes in the best of Hitchcock's movies: a gut-tightening feeling that continued to grow worse until the movie's payoff. But this feeling had no payoff. It just became more intense, more painful, and it meant only one thing...

The sun was rising.

That was when the screaming began outside in the darkness as...

...Phil and Claude Carsey stopped struggling against the ropes that tied them. They sat still and listened to the sounds that were coming from all around outside.

"The fuck is that?" Claude barked, out of breath.

Phil just listened, chest heaving.

It grew even louder and both men felt their scrotums shriveling as they realized what they were hearing.

"It's them," Claude breathed.

"Shit... sunrise."

"What're they doin' out there? How come they ain't found a place to hide? How come they ain't in the trucks?"

"The fuck am I s'posed t'know?"

They listened as it grew louder still, as if it were coming closer...

...closer...

...dangerously close, until—

—it sounded as if it were right outside—

"The window!" Phil cried in a shrill voice.

"Holy shit!" Claude shouted, slamming his back against his brother's, struggling against the ropes. "Get us outta here! Somebody get us outta here for the love of Gaawwwd!"

The brothers fell on their sides and craned their necks to look up at the window, which was completely blocked by a wall of leering faces. They continued screaming for help, begging for rescue, but...

...panic was breaking out in the restaurant and, above the voices of the frightened patrons, no one heard the two men in the basement.

Byron had already loaded his gun with six bloody bullets and was on his feet facing the window shouting, "What the hell's that?"

Bill rose slowly, his entire body tense and aching. "The sun's...coming up," he whispered.

"What's that mean?"

"Means...if they don't...if we don't...find shelter...we're gonna die."

Byron spun on him, shouting, "What the hell you mean, we're gonna—" He froze, staring at Bill, eyes wide, mouth hanging open. From the look on Byron's face, Bill thought it was probably best that he couldn't see himself, but he couldn't resist lifting a hand and touching his cheek.

His skin felt like beef jerky.

Byron looked as if he were about to speak, but no sound came from his mouth; if it did, Bill couldn't hear it above the voices of the crowd. Bill leaned close to him and rasped, "Calm them down. Tell 'em...it's good...what's happening. They're dying out there."

After a moment, Byron turned and shouted, "Hey! Everybody just quiet down, here! C'mon, no, just—" When he realized it wasn't working, he pointed the gun in the air and fired.

The voices fell to a murmur.

"Nobody panic, now, y'hear? What you're hearing out there is good. It means—" He stopped mid-sentence and, along with Bill and everyone else, listened.

It was quiet outside.

"What happened?" Byron whispered.

Just the whining of the wind. And something else, something softer. Voices...muffled, screaming voices...

Bill frowned and rasped, "Sounds like...like it's coming from... from the base—"

"Basement!" Byron shouted. "The fuckin' basement! We forgot to cover the window to the fuckin' basement!"

Byron dashed around Bill toward the hallway that led to the basement door as the crowd's panic began to grow again. Bill fell against the counter and closed his eyes when the realization struck him, his stomach sinking as if it were filled with lead.

The voices belonged to the Carsey Brothers.

The lot lizards had gotten into the building.

Bill knew he wouldn't be the only one who would not see daylight...

CHAPTER 19

Momma'd kick my nigger ass to hell and back, she knew I did some dumb fuck thing like that, Byron thought angrily as he ran across the restaurant toward the rear corridor wondering how he could have possibly neglected to see that garlic was placed outside the basement window as well as all the others. He took his flashlight from his jacket pocket, suddenly aware of the fact that his bowels needed to move.

What had always seemed to be a short, unthreatening corridor seemed to stretch on forever as he moved into deeper and deeper darkness. The closer he got to the basement door, the better he could hear a sound that was coming from the other side, and a few feet from the door, he slowed his pace to a fast walk, listening.

He couldn't make it out yet, but it was not a voice or footsteps. It sounded more like…sloshing.

His keys jangled as he found the master and slipped it into the lock.

The sound continued.

He turned the key and pushed the door open.

The sound became more distinct.

It was wet and thick and came from the darkness below.

Sucking.

The flashlight beam pierced the darkness as it swept down the stairs searching for the source of the sound. The saucer of light passed over a few feet of dirty concrete floor, a couple of crates and—

—a pair of shapely female legs on their knees, then two

more, and slender white arms splashed with black-red and a face smeared with it and—

—Byron tried to gasp but his lungs failed to work as he looked down at the swarm of pale bloody faces that rose quickly from the glistening mess that used to be the Carsey brothers and looked up at him.

He spent a moment in eternity at the top of those stairs, locked in the gaze of dozens of startled eyes glittering in the beam of his flashlight. Byron thought briefly of his mother's smile as a wet throaty hiss rose from below and the girls moved as one toward the stairs. He made a small pathetic sound—not unlike the sound he used to make as a child when he was afraid-—and raised the gun, firing twice into the mass of bloody grinning faces pushing upward toward him, but the gunshots had no effect and the sound he made grew louder as he dropped the flashlight, backed into the corridor and pulled the door shut, clenching his fist around the knob to keep it from being turned from the other side as he screamed down the dark corridor, "Everybody out! Get out of the building! Everybody get out noowwww!"

A chorus of screams erupted in the restaurant. Running feet stormed over the floor in a rush of movement; glass shattered and men and women shouted incoherently.

The knob jiggled in Byron's hand and he tightened his grip, pointed the gun and emptied it into the door. It did no good. Fists pounded the door and the collective hiss from the other side became a guttural snarl.

"Byron!"

Dropping the gun and clutching the doorknob with both hands, Byron looked to the other end of the corridor and saw Bill leaning against the wall unsteadily, holding one of the halogen lanterns at chest level, his face lost in shadow. Behind him, through the windows, Byron could see the first dull ghost of daylight in the iron sky.

"Byron! Come outside! Hurry! They won't last long out there! Just run! "Bill lifted the lantern a bit higher so his face was bathed in its harsh white glow. His pale skin had become dry and flakey, wrinkling deeply around his eyes and mouth.

He looked twenty years older.

Byron opened his mouth to tell Bill to find his wife and kids and go and he would follow, but realized that Bill wouldn't last long out there either and before he could say anything—

—the door cracked and splintered and a bloodied arm shot through the jagged opening, a hand slapped onto the side of Byron's face and closed hard, digging nails into his flesh and slamming his head against the door.

He could hear Bill shouting at him pleadingly, but the voice sounded far away as the hand pulled his head against the door again and again and he released the doorknob, pushing with both hands against the door, trying to pull away from the vice-like grip, but—

—the fingernails had punched through his cheek and the fingers were curled behind his lower teeth, the thumb stabbing upward beneath his jaw, its hold powerful and unrelenting, and—

—Byron screamed as the door opened and the arms slid out of the darkness, embracing him like tentacles, and hands tore at his clothes, fangs ripped his flesh and tongues lapped at his blood.

He fought at first, writhing on the floor, flailing and kicking, but the pain became too great, the screams of his attackers too loud, and as his own blood gurgled in his throat and spattered into his eyes, Byron wondered who would mop up the mess as...

...Bill backed away from the corridor feeling helpless and angry at both himself and Byron. Unable to watch the blood bath a few yards away, he turned toward the panic in the restaurant.

People were running in all directions: some from the restaurant toward the front doors, others from the store into the restaurant calling the names of children and spouses.

Leaning against walls and counters and chairs, Bill walked unsteadily into the chaos holding the lantern up and searching for A.J. and the kids.

On the floor just a few feet in front of him was Jenny Lake. She was huddled protectively over Shawna screaming to no one in particular, "What's happening my God what's happening what's—"

"Take the girl and go, Jenny, just get out of here!" Bill shouted to be heard above the confusion.

She looked up at him, tears streaking her terrified face. "But what's happening, where do we go, where do we—"

Fighting to keep his balance, Bill reached down and gripped her upper arm, pulling hard. "Outside! Get outside!"

Shawna was curled into a fetal position on the floor, now wrapped in her mother's coat rather than using it as a pillow, and her wide eyes darted around in the dim light, confused and terrified. Jenny slid her arms under the frail little girl and scooped her up off the floor.

"Hold it," Bill said, putting the lantern on the coffee counter. He removed his jacket with stiff, weak movements and draped it over Jenny's shoulders. "It's even colder out there," he said, nodding toward the exit.

Jenny made a sound that might have been meant as a thank you, but in Bill's ringing ears it was nothing more than a grunt. She turned and shouldered her way into the crowd and, as they hurried out, Shawna looked at Bill over her mother's shoulder and, realizing that he wasn't following them, shouted, "Bill! C'mon, come with us!"

Bill lifted his lantern again and waved at the girl. "I'll be fine."

"No! Mommy, wait for Bill!"

They disappeared into the crowd.

Bill turned back to the corridor and squinted into the darkness. He could only see shadowy movements, but he could hear enough: horrible slurping and sucking, like pigs in mud. When they were finished, would they be daring enough to follow everyone outside in spite of the threat of sunrise? Were they that crazed?

Maybe.

He turned and began shouting, "A.J.! Dara! Cece! Jonny!" He walked into the fleeing crowd calling their names over and over. A woman with silver hair bumped into him as she spun around, shouting at everyone who rushed past her, "Stop it!

Stop this right now!" Her eyes were wide with the look of one who has abandoned her sanity. She waved her fists in the air. "I am the manager! I am responsible! Stop this right now!"

"Come on, ma'am," Bill said, taking her arm and trying to turn her toward the front of the building. "You've got to get out of here, it's danger—"

She lashed out and caught him hard in the ribs with her forearm, screaming through clenched teeth, "Get your hands off of me! I'm the manager, goddammit!"

The world tilted and Bill's head struck the edge of a table as he fell. He dropped the lantern and it rolled over the floor away from him. His mouth opened and he tried to cry out in pain, but could not find his voice. He watched through bleary eyes as legs rushed by him; feet kicked him and stepped on his arms and legs and garbled voices faded slowly, as if he were sinking under water.

You're dying already...

...dying already...

...already...already...

Bill closed his eyes and waited for the final deadly silence and the everlasting sleep of death to descend as...

.. Jon jerked his arm from Doug's grasp and shouted, "Let me go! I'm gonna go back and help my dad!"

They were just a few feet from the entrance, which was clogged with people pushing one another aside to get out. Doug stood between Jon and Dara, holding each by the elbow, while Mom stood in front of them holding Cece's hand. When Jon pulled away and shouted at Doug, Dara and Cece turned to him abruptly.

"Dad's here?" Dara asked urgently.

Cece pulled on her mother's arm. "Where's Dad, Mom? Where is he?"

Jon could tell by the sinking expression on his mom's face that she hadn't planned on telling the girls that his dad was around.

Doug took his arm again and said firmly, "He can take care of himself, Jon, now let's—"

"He's sick!" Jon screamed, pulling away again and turned to go back into the restaurant.

"What'samatter with Daddy, Mom?" Cece asked, still tugging her arm as Dara asked simultaneously, "Is Dad really sick, Mother? Is he?"

Doug clutched Jon's shoulders from behind and pulled him out of the way of an enormous fat woman holding a baby and blubbering senselessly as she rushed by, shoving people aside roughly to get to the doors. Doug held him close, wrapping an arm around Jon's chest and half dragging him through the first set of glass doors, growling, "You can all see your dad when we get outside, okay? Outside!"

Bilious anger burned in Jon's throat and he began kicking back at Doug's shins and digging his elbows into Doug's abdomen to get away; he accidentally kicked an elderly woman whose husband was helping her out of the building, but they didn't stick around for an apology.

Jon shouted, "He can't go outside, you sonofabitch! The sun'll kill him!" He broke free and spun to face them, his breath coming fast and hard.

The girls stared at him in shocked confusion, jerking back and forth as they were bumped and jostled by others hurrying out.

"You can go outside if you want," Jon said, backing into the store, "but I'm gonna see if I can help him."

Dara turned to her mother: "We can't leave him, Mom."

Cece began to bob up and down slightly, as if she had to urinate: "We gotta help Daddy! I wanna see him! Please, let's help him!"

Jon watched as a long, silent look passed between Mom and Doug, then Doug sighed, "Take the girls outside, Adelle." To Jon: "Let's go."

Jon's tight shoulders relaxed with relief so strong that he almost laughed out loud as he turned and headed back toward the restaurant.

There were still more people coming out, some of them taking advantage of the chaos and ducking into the store to do a little last minute looting, others lagging behind with children or bags they'd brought in with them. A few lanterns remained scattered around the dark restaurant; the last ones leaving the restaurant were either limping or being helped out, having been injured in the initial panic. A silver haired woman stood in the middle of the darkness pounding her fist on a table and shouting, "You are all going to lose your fucking jobs, every last one of you, and I am not going to be responsible, do you hear me?" Her voice was raw and hoarse and her body moved in rigid, nervous jerks, her knees nearly buckling now and then as her legs quaked. The last waitress in the room went to her side, murmuring soothingly as she tried to put her arm around the woman's shoulders. The woman jerked away, shouting, "You are fired as of now, missy, do you understand? Get your things and get out of here!" The waitress backed up reluctantly, then hurried out, crying. The woman turned, then, and pointed at the floor to her left: "And some body get this God damned drunk off the floor and out of here!"

Jon spotted him. He was sprawled on the floor on his back. And he was holding very, very still.

"Dad!" he shouted, hurrying toward him with Doug beside him.

But the crazy woman was faster, rushing to his side and pulling back her leg to kick him, growling, "Goddamned transient wino!"

Jon sprinted forward and dove, barking, "No!" as he tackled her to the floor.

The woman landed on the carpet but rolled to the strip of tile floor that ran behind the counter. Stunned, she propped herself up on her side just a few feet from the entrance to a dark corridor as Jon crawled on hands and knees to his dad's side.

"My God," Doug breathed as he looked down at him.

Dad looked even worse than he had just a short while ago. His white, flakey skin was shriveled and seemed to be running off his skull like melting wax. His hair had become coarse and his fingernails were darkened slightly. The appearance was not that of age, but of decay, of rot.

Jon's heart sank. Tears stung his eyes and blurred the face that no longer resembled his father's.

Doug knelt and touched two fingertips to his throat. "He

doesn't have a pulse," he said quietly. "And he's not breathing."

"Course not!" Jon sobbed. "He's been dead for over a year!" Jon grabbed his dad's shoulders and shook him hard. "Dad! Dad, you gotta wake up! We're gonna help you outta here, Dad! Dad!"

Doug touched Jon's arm and said gently, "Doug, that's not going to do any good. There's nothing we can—"

"Sun…" The word was spoken in a paper-thin voice through cracked and peeling lips that barely moved.

"Dad?"

"The sun…is coming…up…"

Doug stared at the body, horrified.

Jon leaned close to him. "What should we do, Dad? Tell us what to do!"

Bills eyelids peeled open slowly and his dulled, sunken eyes tried hard to focus until they found Jon's face. "Jonny…"

"Whatta we do?"

"Girls…safe?"

Jon nodded.

"Mom?"

Again.

When Jon saw that his dad was trying feebly to sit up, he and Doug helped him, one on each side. Bill groaned and squinted as he looked toward the window. Outside, the grey sky had grown just a bit lighter, but darkness still ruled.

"Truck," Bill coughed.

"What?"

"Take me…to my truck…where it's…dark…"

"He wants to go to his truck," Jon said.

Doug nodded, his features curled with disgust. "Okay, let's get him—"

"I'm going to report all of you!"

They both tossed a glance at the woman. She was sitting up now, her shoulders slumped, her face sagging and slick with tears. She spoke to no one in particular, just sat there with legs spread before her, stiff arms propping her up, head lolling as she cried.

"Report every…damned…one of you…"

"Okay, let's get him up," Doug said.

Jon turned back to his dad, but only for an instant; something had caught his eye and he turned to the woman again. Something moved in the darkness of the corridor behind her. Something white. Several somethings.

Arms. Long arms reached out slowly, silently.

And faces. White, geisha-like faces smeared with...with something, each with two deep black holes from which sinister eyes glistened.

They moved forward, arms outstretched, slowly at first, and then—

—they pounced. The arms wrapped around the woman and the faces opened sloppy, smeared mouths with fangs that dripped of dark fluids and the woman's face showed only a heartbeat of surprise before—

—the arms pulled her into the darkness and all Jon could see were her legs, kicking silently and uselessly, and then—

—the darkness was just darkness again, except for the horrible sucking sounds that began...

"Doug!" Jon shouted.

He'd seen it, too. "Holy shit," he barked, lifting Bill clumsily and shouting, "Out! Get outta here!"

Faces appeared in the darkness again, moving out of the corridor and into the glare of the halogen lanterns, three of them, looking directly at Jon and—

—smiling.

Doug bundled Bill in his arms as easily as if he were a sack of laundry and Jon followed him out, glancing over his shoulder as the women became fully visible now, their clothes hanging in tatters on their bloody bodies, a white red-splashed breast exposed here, a spattered thigh there.

"Hurry," Bill rasped. "God...hurry..."

Doug and Jon broke into a run, slowing for no one and nothing, knocking over a display of greeting cards as they rounded the corner and pushed out the first set of glass doors, then knocking an ashtray over before getting through the second.

It was still snowing outside, harder than ever, and people

were standing in the parking lot, some speaking in hushed tones and watching the building expectantly, while others huddled together a few feet away and continued singing hymns.

"Daddy?" Cece screamed from somewhere in the crowd. "Is that Daddy? Daddeeee!"

"No!" Adelle shouted, her voice thick with emotion. "Stay here, Cece, just wait here." She caught up with them as they ran across the parking lot toward Bill's truck across the street. "My God, what's wrong?" she cried. "What's happening to him?"

Jon saw that he was getting worse; his cheeks were more hollow and his arms shook. But even more disturbing was the expression of pain and fear on his face—eyes closed tightly, lips quivering—and the thin whimpering sound he made. When he spoke, his voice was forced and unsteady.

"The girls...stay with the girls," Bill said, turning his face toward Adelle without opening his eyes.

They stopped beside the truck and Doug said, "He's right, Adelle, go back with the girls. I'll be over in a minute. And get everybody away from the building. Thuh-those-those things are in there."

She protested at first and tried to talk to Bill, but Doug convinced her and she headed back reluctantly.

"Inside...puh-please," Bill hissed and Doug opened the cab and carried him inside as Jon followed. Doug lifted him into the dark sleeper where he curled into a ball and groaned, "The ice... box...in the corner..."

Jon was smaller, so he crawled up into the sleeper, squinted in the darkness and found the icebox in the corner at the foot of the bed. He opened it to find several plastic bags stacked in rows. Each was filled with a thick dark red liquid.

He winced when he realized what it was and just knelt there staring at the bags for a while.

"Juh-Jonny, please..." Dad groaned.

With twitching fingers, he reached into the icebox and removed one of the bags, holding the corner gingerly between thumb and forefinger as he turned to his father.

Bill snatched the bag from Jon's hand and began to tear at the top clumsily with his teeth, holding it in convulsing hands.

"C'mon, Dad, you don't need that," Jon said quietly, pleadingly. "We'll get you a doctor and he can—"

Bill just waved a hand, dismissing him, as the bag ripped open. He tipped it back and opened its mouth, letting the thick blood ooze between his swollen, cracked lips. Some of it dribbled down his chin as he gulped loudly, stopping to cough once and lick his lips.

Jon's stomach hitched and he turned away so quickly he almost fell out of the sleeper. He stumbled down into the passenger seat and leaned forward, holding his face in his hands, feeling sick, hoping that someday he would be able to forget what had happened in the last night and, most of all, what he had just seen. Doug patted his back helplessly as...

...Bill experienced a faint shadow of the feeling that had once been better than the best sex. He dropped the empty bag and shuddered, his tongue smacking around the corners of his mouth as he laid back and struggled to feel the blood warming him, enriching him, filling the rotting, decaying holes that he could imagine were opening up deep inside him. But the effect was minimal and short lived. Bill lay in the dark, eyes closed, listening to the muffled whispers of Doug and Jon in the cab.

Full daylight would arrive very soon. He could feel it coming in his bones. In fact, the reason he trembled so was because daylight was too close. That and, of course, other reasons.

You're dying already...already...already...

The creatures hiding in the darkness of the truck stop would retreat to the basement and huddle in some dark corner until the sun was gone again and they could come out to feed. But they would probably no longer try to hide; now that their queen was gone, they would no doubt abandon all subtlety and attack their victims ravenously as they had been doing since that creature had crumbled to black mud in the restaurant.

But until the next night, they would be vulnerable.

Until dusk, they would remain in the truck stop.

Easy targets.

If he waited too long, though, he would be an easy target, too.

"Jon," Bill rasped, his voice a little stronger but not much.

After a moment: "Yeah?"

Sitting up, Bill wiped his bloody face on a blanket. "Come here, please."

Jon was reluctant, but he peered over the edge of the bed, never meeting Bill's eyes.

"Do me a favor," Bill said, trying to keep his voice steady. "Go out there with your mom, okay?"

He said nothing.

"And… guh-give your sisters a… a hug from me. Tell them I love them and I'm sorry I didn't get to see them. Maybe…maybe some other time."

Jon started to turn away, muttering, "Liar."

Bill grabbed his wrist and held him. "I'm sorry, Jonny. You know I didn't… want any of this to happen. It's just one of those things. Life's full of them. Nobody's at fault. Nothing anybody can do. If you can't stop hating me…at least don't take it out on your mother. And on Doug. Okay?"

Still averting his eyes, the boy nodded only slightly.

Bill wanted to ask him for a hug, but he didn't want to do that to the boy. Instead, he just looked at him in the dark, went over Jon's face slowly with his eyes, recording every feature, every flaw. And he saw something he'd never noticed before. It was on Jon's neck, below his jaw. A small patch of skin beneath which something lurked.

It was a wonderful thing…

Unless you feed on living humans…

… a beautiful thing…

…unless you drink warm blood still pumping through human veins and arteries…

…a seductive thing.

…you will die.

It was a pulse.

You're dying already.

Bill jerked his head away and tried not to think about that pulse, about that fresh, pumping blood, or about the gnawing burning hunger that flared in his gut. He squeezed Jon's wrist and said in a strained voice, "I…love you…son."

Jon broke then. His face crumbled into a mask of pain and

he quickly sobbed, "Me, too," as he dropped out of sight and hurried out of the truck.

Bill took a moment to gather as much strength as he could find and sat up, hanging his legs off the bed. Fat snowflakes still fell from steel-colored clouds, the bottoms of which glowed ever so softly. Daylight was brighter but still very young, yet it fired scalding shards of metal into Bill's eyes and he shielded them with a hand. Doug sat in the passenger seat looking up at him with a mixture of apprehension and helplessness.

"Is there anything I can do, Bill?" he asked nervously.

"Yeah. Grab my sunglass out of that pouch on the door." Doug handed him the glasses and he put them on. They helped some, but not much. In a few minutes, they wouldn't help at all and Bill knew he would be useless, a corpse rotting quickly in the dull, clouded sunlight. "Now," Bill said, "go out there and get everybody as far away from the building as possible."

"Why?"

He shook his head. "Just do it. And, um…take care of A.J. and the kids. Take good care of them. And tell A.J.…." Tell her what? he thought. Why tell her anything? "…tell her how sorry I am."

"Look, Bill, maybe there's something we can do, somebody who can help you take care of this and get bet—"

"Just go."

Doug nodded slowly, opened the door and got out. He stood outside for a moment, watching Bill.

"Hurry, dammit!"

The door slammed and Bill heard Doug's footsteps crunching over the snow. He watched him head back to the crowd in the parking lot. An off-key, muddled rendition of "The Old Rugged Cross" came from one corner of the parking lot, sung by unsteady, frightened voices. To the right of the building, he could see part of the truck lot and, even with bleary eyes, he could see several still bodies sprawled on the snowy ground here and there. Then his eyes turned to the gas island, to the pumps standing like mechanical guards beneath the white steel canopy, lined up with their curved chrome fingers stuck in their ears.

It might not work. The power was out, which lessened his chances. But there were three cars still parked by the pumps, cars that had no doubt been there filling up when the power went off and had been left there so the drivers could finish the job when it came back on. If it failed, there was always the diesel island. Whether it worked or not, he had to try. After all…

You're dying already…

CHAPTER 20

As Doug neared the crowd in front of the truck stop, he was overcome with exhaustion. He felt as if he'd lived a whole month—a very bad one—in just one night, and although she was crying and chewing her lip, her arms around the girls, both of whom were also crying, it was comforting to see Adelle's face. He opened his arms to her and she fell into them, sobbing.

"What's wrong with him?" she asked.

"I'm not sure, but…well, he's…" He chuckled without humor, unable to believe what he was saying, "…he's one of them. One of those things. And he's…very sick. I guess. Hell, I don't know. Jon says he's been dead for a year."

Adelle closed her eyes and turned away, her lips thinning as she held back more tears.

"Sorry, honey. He's resting right now." He reached out and massaged her shoulders, frowning. It hurt him to see Adelle so moved and upset by Bill's condition. It was immature and petty, he knew; they had, after all, been married and had three children together. But seeing her emotion for her ex-husband—the man of whom she'd said so many bitter things since Doug had been with her—unsettled something in him, made him feel insecure. Shaking his head abruptly, trying to dismiss his feelings, he embraced her again, held her in silence for a moment. He turned to Jon, who stood a few feet away, watching his dad's truck, eyes red and swollen, lips quivering. "You okay, Jon?" He nodded.

"We wanna see him!" Cece cried.

Doug hunched down and stroked her face. "You can't see him, sweetheart. Not right now. He's very sick and he just needs to rest. Maybe later." But he knew that wasn't going to happen.

Not if he could help it. He kissed Adelle and moved toward the noisy crowd. They were cold and frightened and still unsure of what they'd been through. He lifted his arms and called, "Um, excuse me, folks. Could I have your attention?"

Heads turned to him slowly, a few at a time, and he repeated himself, then said, "Um, we don't think those... those, uh, things will be coming out after sunrise, and it's almost light now. But until then, it's probably a good idea to move away from the building. If we could all just move over here by the street? The freeway should be open soon and maybe we'll get some help in here. I think if we just—"

An engine roared to life.

"He's starting his truck!" Jon shouted.

Doug spun around and saw the lights on Bill's Kenworth come on, saw Bill turn to them, just staring through his sunglasses for a while.

"What the hell's he doing?" Doug muttered.

The crowd fell silent and everyone watched the blue tractor across the street.

"He can't drive," Jon said. "Not as sick as he is. Mom, somebody's gotta stop him." He started toward the street, but Doug grabbed his arm.

"Uh-uh. Just sit tight."

The engine idled for a while.

The sky grew lighter.

The snow continued to fall.

Then the tractor moved. It drove forward slowly then veered left as if to make a U-turn. But it didn't. It kept going straight. The grill clattered as it tore through the hedges surrounding the parking lot and took out part of the truck stops old wooden roadside sign.

Voices rose, some in anger, some in fear.

Doug's mouth became dry very suddenly. "Son of a bitch," he breathed.

The Kenworth's horn wailed once, twice, a third time as it picked up speed, nicking the back end of a small pickup that was sloppily parked; the pickup spun away from it and the horn didn't stop this time, just kept wailing, screaming.

Doug turned to see where the truck was headed and he didn't wait a heartbeat to scream, "Run! Everybody run! Into the street! Now!" He swept Cece up under one arm and pushed Adelle ahead of him; she dragged Dara at her side.

But Jon just stood and watched, his jaw slack.

"Dammit, Jonny, come on!" Doug shouted.

The others ran, some fell and crawled until they regained their footing; a few were trampled before they got back up. Screams rose in the quiet snowy dawn as...

...Jonny backed up, slowly at first, his eyes following the Kenworth in which his prize Triceratops dangled in the window. He kept his eye on his dad's window, watching as his head bobbed while the tractor gained speed. He backed up faster, breaking into an awkward jog as it neared the gas island, heading straight for the first row of pumps. There was a split second, just an instant, when Jon saw his dad's head turn to look out the window; the sunglasses were crooked on his face and his mouth was a gaping black hole framing a silent scream.

Then Jon ran, crying and screaming.

And hell came out of the pavement.

The explosion made a deafening gushing sound and its impact carried Jon several feet, throwing him into the shrubs, where he struggled to stand and continue running. He didn't want to look back, didn't want to see his father's fate.

But he had to.

On his feet again, he turned around and continued running backward, his feet sliding dangerously over the icy pavement.

The biggest, angriest flames Jon had ever seen were engulfing his dad's Kenworth and shooting into the sky. Black smoke billowed up to meet the clouds. The canopy that had covered the pumps fell through the air gracefully, almost as if it were falling in slow motion, and landed on several cars in the lot with a thunderous crash.

There was another smaller explosion, this one from under the main building, half of which disappeared sending missiles of rubble into the air. Even across the street, Jon could feel the heat enough to make his skin tingle and his eyes burn and water.

The diesel island went next and another steel canopy was

lifted on a wave of fire and came down on a row of trucks parked in the truck lot.

The others who had fled the building had scattered in every direction and almost all of them had hit the ground, either for protection or from the concussion of the explosion; some of them were in the street, others in the bushes or sprawled in a snowbank. Their cries and screams and panicked babbling served as music for the fire's ballet.

But Jon couldn't speak or make a sound. He just stood in the middle of the street, in one spot, and turned very slowly around and around as bits of pavement and metal and charred wood rained from the sky, and no matter where he looked, no matter what he saw, the most vivid image in his eyes was that of his father's decaying face, sunglasses askew, screaming soundlessly as he drove to his death.

Through their tears, some of the people had, once again, begun to sing a hymn as they gathered together across the street: "Blessed Assurance."

Jon's mother rushed to him, embraced him and kissed him again and again, whispering his name. Still holding him close, she led him across the street to where Dara and Cece pressed their faces into Doug's side, sobbing and trying to keep warm.

The five of them stood close as another sound rose above the cries and roar of the flames. It sounded, at first, like a strong gust of wind sighing through tall pines. Gradually, the scattered crowd calmed a bit, tense perhaps, afraid of what might be coming next. Heads turned from right to left, looking for the source of the sound, which was joined by another, and a third. The sounds grew louder, clashing with the hymn singers, whose voices faltered and finally stopped as all eyes turned toward the mountain of fire that had once been the Sierra Gold Pan Truck Stop.

They were screams. ..unearthly, agonizing screams rising from the blaze, only to fade away again until all that was left was the roar of the fire...

EPILOGUE

Amy sat up suddenly, her sticky eyes fluttering several times before opening completely. All she knew upon waking was that she was ravenous. Her body ached for a feeding; her head throbbed and her joints were stiff. Worst of all, she had no idea where she was or what was tangling her legs together. She reached down and pulled it away to find that it was a frayed green canvas. It smelled damp and moldy. In fact, everything around her smelled damp and moldy.

She looked around at old wooden walls on which hung two rakes, a shovel, a hoe and an axe. When she tried to stand, her back bumped into something and she glanced over her shoulder at a neatly stacked pile of firewood.

And something else.

Something attached to her back. She tried to stand but dizziness plopped her back down on the creaky wooden floor. Even after the dizziness passed, she could not keep her balance and dropped on her ass two more times. She tried to reach behind her to see what was weighing her down, but she noticed that her clothes were hanging from her body in tatters and she froze.

Groaning, she closed her eyes and put her head in her palms, sliding her fingers into her wet, matted hair.

The last thing she remembered was rushing from the truck stop basement with Kevin to his truck in the parking lot. No… no, there was more…

They left the truck stop to go…where? Kevin's place, yes, that was it. He was going to get a few things, put his camper shell on his pick-up and, as soon as the weather improved a little, they were going to hit the road.

Driving through the snow: that was the last thing she remembered. Or was there something else...

The pain. Yes, the pain that had struck her like a snake. Flames had scorched the inside of her skull; thinking back on it now, she could imagine her brain boiling like water in a kettle left too long on a stove. She vaguely remembered how frightened Kevin was as he struggled to keep the pick-up on the road. At first, she'd thought it was because she was putting distance between herself and the queen; she'd tried it before, always with painful results. But the pain she'd had in Kevin's pickup had been worse than anything she'd ever experienced, and when it continued to grow worse, she'd realized it was being caused by something else, something much more permanent than the distance between herself and the queen.

She remembered what that pain had driven her to do, too. Smacking her lips, she could still detect the bitter, stale taste of Kevin's blood on her tongue. She tried to feel remorse—he'd been a nice enough boy, so eager to help her, to be with her— but she couldn't; it simply wasn't there. In fact, when she went deep inside herself looking for that remorse, she realized that something else was missing, too.

The queen.

She'd always been there; Amy had never been without the queen's presence since she'd been bled. But now she was gone.

The psychic tie that had always connected her to that creature in the trailer had been cut.

A smile moved slowly across Amy's face and she whispered in the dark, "She's dead."

She was free. She didn't have to run anymore.

Amy leaned over to the wall and looked through a crack between two of the wooden slats. It was dark outside. The day was gone. She'd escaped sunrise in time.

With an enthusiasm she couldn't remember feeling since she was a child, Amy stood again, remained upright for a few moments, then began to sway backward. She slapped her hands onto the wall and held herself up. Reaching her left arm over her shoulder, she touched her fingertips to something. It was attached to her back just above her shoulder blade.

There was one on the other side, too.

She shook her shoulders, hoping to dislodge the objects from her back. There was a hushed rustling sound behind her, a stirring of the cold air around her, but the weight on her back remained. Frowning, Amy looked down at herself, surveying the damage to her clothes. And then, even in the darkness, she saw it.

A fine layer of dark hair over her entire body. She ran her hand over her breasts in disbelief, but held the hand out before her when she noticed how long her nails had become. How long and black.

"Oh, my God," she said aloud, and her voice was different. Slightly muffled. Her mouth felt funny...full. She touched her face and—

—her mouth was swollen, sticking out from her face, almost like...like a muzzle.

"Oh, my God," she said again, her voice a whine now. It was as if a veil had been lifted from her eyes and, now that she was fully awake, she realized that her entire body felt different... and that the things on her back would not come off. They would never come off.

Not me...not me...I'll never become like that....not me...

Clumsily, Amy spread her new wings.

Her stomach twisted and she leaned over, as if to vomit, then dropped to her knees, her face in her hands, and sobbed.

Not me...not me...

She swallowed her tears when she heard a sound outside.

A door opening.

Stomping feet.

A girl's voice, early teens, maybe younger: "I'm doing it now, Dad, I am getting the wood! Jeez!"

The door slammed and footsteps crunched through the snow as the voice mumbled indignantly: "...always following orders...like bein' in the fucking Army, for cryin' out...do this, do that...good ol' Kunta Kinte, that's me, yes massah, no massah..."

Crunch-crunch, crunch-crunch... louder, closer...

Amy's crying stopped and was forgotten in seconds. She

could smell the girl, she could feel her pulse already, feel it in her bones.

She stood, moved to the door of the wood shed and spread her wings again.

There was no time to hate herself now, no time to mourn her condition.

There was her hunger to appease...there was blood to drink...

...there were places to go...

ABOUT THE AUTHOR

Ray Garton has been writing novels, novellas, short stories, and essays for more than 30 years. His work spans the genres of horror, crime, suspense, and even comedy. Live Girls was nominated for the Bram Stoker Award in 1988, and Garton received the Grand Master of Horror Award at the 2006 World Horror Convention. He lives in northern California with his wife Dawn, where he is at work on a new novel.

Curious about other Crossroad Press books?
Stop by our site:
http://store.crossroadpress.com
We offer quality writing
in digital, audio, and print formats.